# SINLESS

# SINLESS

## EYE OF THE BEHOLDER

### BOOK 1

## sarah tarkoff

HARPER Voyager
*An Imprint of* HarperCollins*Publishers*

SINLESS. Copyright © 2018 by Sarah Tarkoff. All rights reserved. Printed in the United States of America. No part of this book may be used or reproduced in any manner whatsoever without written permission except in the case of brief quotations embodied in critical articles and reviews. For information, address HarperCollins Publishers, 195 Broadway, New York, NY 10007.

HarperCollins books may be purchased for educational, business, or sales promotional use. For information, please email the Special Markets Department at SPsales@harpercollins.com.

FIRST EDITION

Harper Voyager and design are trademarks of HarperCollins Publishers LLC.

Designed by Joy O'Meara

Library of Congress Cataloging-in-Publication Data has been applied for.

ISBN 978-0-06-245638-0

18 19 20 21 22    LSC    10 9 8 7 6 5 4 3 2 1

For my parents, all of you

# SINLESS

*Many of you hate me. I'd hate me, if I were you.*

*I made decisions that hurt a lot of you. That killed people you loved. I could say I was in over my head, that I tried my best, but that would be making excuses, and that's not what you're looking for. You want an apology. A big fat apology, an admission that I messed everything up. And I'm sorry, I genuinely am, for all of it.*

*So what am I hoping for from you? Forgiveness? No, I can't imagine I'll get that. Understanding, that's really all I want. Because looking back now, I know I should have done better. But I didn't, and I want you to understand why.*

*For that reason, I want to present this narrative as I experienced it. I want to convey my point of view at that time, as naïve as it may seem now. I've done my best to re-create moments and dialogue as accurately as possible, despite how long ago they happened. I believe this is a story that needs to be told, and I hope you're willing to listen. I have great faith in humanity, and in Great Spirit, and in our collective ability to work together to move forward.*

> *With all the love of Great Spirit,*
> *Grace Luther*
> *c/o Arlington Federal Prison*

# PROLOGUE

That day. We were in Jude's pickup, careening down one of those rural Virginia roads with a dotted yellow line down the middle. Sheer cliffs winding up a mountain, beautiful in a precarious kind of way.

Who was Jude? You've never heard of him, but he's the reason you've heard of me. He's the reason all of this started.

Jude was my next-door neighbor, childhood best friend, and frequent Super Soaker victim. When I was five and he was six, his parents gave him this red stuffed bear with a recording device in its stomach. You pressed a button, and it would repeat whatever you said. Since this was pre-Revelation, we giggled to hear it say "poop" and "fart," the dirtiest words we knew in preschool, and I whined at my parents until they got me a matching blue one. We traded them back and forth, recording secret messages.

But by the time we got to high school, everything had changed. Sure, Jude was cute—he was nice, and all nice guys were cute—but he was gawky and shy, always wearing some too-formal button-down his mom had laid out for him. He'd come up to me in the hall with long-winded stories, and I'd watch my friends' eyes glaze over. I never said a mean thing to his face, but when he left, I'd join in their giggling. "Jude looooooves you," they'd tease. They'd mock how nervous he seemed around me, and I went right along with it, glad for the ego boost. I always wondered why I wasn't Punished for my disloyalty, my unkindness.

Despite my sophomoric behavior, our friendship continued, grew. I'd leave that old blue bear on my windowsill, and he'd sneak up and elocute into its belly these long, thought-out dissertations on world events, pop culture, whatever intrigued him that day. And the truth is, away from the judging eyes of my friends, I really did think he was one of the most intelligent, funniest people I'd ever met.

Had things been different, I think in time I would have come around. He would have asked me to prom, I would have said yes, my palms would have gotten sweaty in his as we swayed on the gym floor, and I would have wondered, what is this feeling? And when he kissed me, I would have known. And in our mutual, not-that-special way, we would have gotten married and had lots of babies and taught them to glorify Great Spirit. But instead, on that chilly almost-spring morning, we took a drive.

We were on our way to some youth rally in D.C., nauseatingly wholesome stuff. I still remember everything about that day. The way Jude's hair blew as one funny-looking entity, long overdue for a haircut. How his arms were bigger than I recalled, his jaw squarer, with a hint of a five-o'clock shadow. I remember the moment I realized my best friend had become this handsome man, and I wondered if anyone else had noticed. I remember the way he smiled, the way it lit up the whole car, and I wondered why now, at the age of sixteen, he seemed so different, despite being entirely the same. And how his differentness and his sameness, together, created a feeling I couldn't quite articulate.

I was wearing a hat of my mother's, one she'd crocheted herself. Jude was teasing me about it, maybe to be flirty in his unpracticed way. "It's too small for you."

"It is not! I have a lot of hair," I insisted.

"That's what I mean. Look, it's coming off."

He grabbed for it, and I shrieked. "Stop it!"

He perched the small hat on top of his big head. "See, much better."

"It is not. You look stupid." I grabbed the hat back, but now I couldn't get it to sit correctly on my kinky black curls. I stared at myself in the mirror, trying to readjust.

Jude saw I was unhappy and offered, "I'm kidding! It looks good."

"I don't believe you."

He leaned over and moved the hat just a fraction of an inch, right back into place. I smiled.

"See? You're beautiful." He'd said it without thinking, I think. I looked over at him, and he turned back to the road, a little embarrassed. I was used to people telling me I was beautiful, but there was something about the way he said it . . . and the fact that it was him, it was Jude . . . I desperately wanted him to say it again.

But he kept his focus on the road, quickly adding, for safety, "Only in that hat. Usually you're disgusting." And then a playful smile. But he couldn't fool me. That word, "beautiful"—it was out there.

But I was too timid to confront him directly, so I kept it light. "I never knew you thought I was disgusting."

Jude chuckled, going along with my joke. "That's what all the guys say in the locker room. Grace Luther, super disgusting."

"But none of those guys are you. I mean, none of those guys are my best friend."

Jude stole a glance over at me. "So I'm special."

"Of course you are," I said. Silence filled the car. I couldn't read his expression. In that moment, I rethought everything. What if his awkwardness around me was just awkwardness? What if he didn't have some big crush? Maybe the feelings I'd imagined him having were merely my own invention, because I'd always had a subconscious crush on him. Had I said too much? Had I just ruined our friendship? I quickly added, "Sorry, I didn't mean to . . ."

"No," he said, "I mean, at some point, I wanted to ask you . . ." He paused, trying to find the right words, and in a split second I imagined a hundred different possible outcomes. But out of that hundred, not a single one came close to what happened next.

It took us just that split second to speed around the corner, down a hill—where there was a sedan approaching, straddling both lanes.

Jude slammed on the brakes.

"Honk!" I screamed. But that just panicked him more. The sedan swerved, but it all happened so fast and—

The collision. Metal everywhere. Glass everywhere. Airbags deployed—I couldn't breathe.

Jude's truck skidded for such a long time, I was sure we were headed over the cliff.

I screamed and I prayed, the only two weapons I had, as the squeal of our tires deafened me. *Please, Great Spirit, protect me.*

And He did. We skidded to a stop, inches from the edge of the cliff.

It took me a moment to realize it was over. I punched at my inflated airbag. I couldn't see anything. I tried to reach Jude, but he was so far away, and so quiet. "Jude?" Still nothing. The sound of my own panicked breathing overwhelmed me. Oh no . . . My hands felt for him, finally found his chest.

"Grace? Are you okay?"

And there he was, reaching for me, holding me. His arms had never surrounded me like that before. I remember taking his hand, feeling the slickness of the blood on it. "It's okay. I'm here. I've got you," he said.

I started crying. Held him tight. In that moment, I wanted to take back every time I'd joked with my friends about how geeky he was, I wanted to just pray my thanks forever and ever and ever. And then he looked out through the shattered windshield. He blanched, and he jumped out of the car. I followed.

We hadn't gone off the cliff. We were lucky.

The sedan was ten or twenty feet below the cliff edge, on its side. We heard the sirens coming—our crash had been automatically registered with emergency services—but Jude didn't wait for them to arrive. He jumped down the craggy rocks, toward the car.

"Jude, wait. It's not safe."

But he didn't listen. I scrambled down after him, wondering—

had Jude been speeding? Maybe a little. But I saw him do everything he could to avoid that sedan. Whatever we saw in that other car, it couldn't be his fault.

Through the passenger window, we saw a woman in her thirties, unconscious. Jude peered in at her. "She's breathing." A sigh of relief. And then Jude made that noise. A brief, horrified gasp. I followed his line of sight to the backseat, where a young boy lay in a pool of blood. He couldn't have been more than five, six. His head rested against the window, and something about it wasn't shaped right; it conformed too easily to the glass. His skull had been crushed, I realized with horror. He wasn't moving, wasn't breathing. I stared at that boy, waiting for any sign of movement. Hoping there'd be any chance that when the ambulances arrived, they'd be able to save him. But the longer I looked, the more I was sure that hope was in vain.

I started crying, grabbed on to Jude. And then Jude couldn't hold me up. Startled, I pulled away.

I'm sure you've all guessed what's coming next, but it was the first time I'd seen it in person, so it was a shock to me. I was expecting ugly, but this—it was more than ugly. I remember every detail of how Jude's face twisted, bloating asymmetrically, the color changes—purplish, greenish, yellowish. How the eyes I'd just been staring into bulged, how his tongue hung out. And when I could barely recognize him, how he grabbed at his throat, wheezing, gasping for breath. I could see his windpipe contorting, the skin on his neck straining around it. He fell to his knees, as his muscles grew weak and his throat closed. Jude was being Punished.

I dropped to the ground next to him, hands together, begging, "Please spare him, Great Spirit." I thought if Great Spirit had given me any talent, it was this one—it was bringing faith to someone in a moment of need. This was the one skill a cleric's daughter like me had spent her life honing. I grabbed his hands, put them between mine. "Pray with me," I implored him. "Great Spirit will spare you if you pray with me." He looked at me, doubtful, but I wouldn't be deterred. "You have to try. Please."

I think, though he couldn't talk, he tried. He listened as I said a Hebrew prayer that began with *"baruch atah adonai"* that I'd heard his mother say, a Buddhist mantra, anything I thought Great Spirit might listen to. But his skin kept turning that deathly blue color, and soon, no breath emerged from him at all. His eyes closed. I shook him, I screamed at him, but he'd stopped responding.

I kept praying as the EMTs swarmed around us, putting the woman and her child on stretchers. And as I cried, the EMTs tore me out of Jude's arms. I begged them to let me keep praying, keep trying, but . . .

"He's gone, honey," a kind-eyed EMT said to me gently as Jude, too, disappeared into an ambulance, and I clung to her as it sped away. Her words echoed in my head: Jude was gone. As gone as the little boy in the back of that car. That was Great Spirit's justice. An eye for every eye. Whatever mistakes Jude had made on the road, he paid for them with his life.

No sinner is safe from the wrath of Great Spirit.

# BOOK
## ONE

# CHAPTER 1

Where were you? That's the question everyone asks. *Where were you when you were Converted? What country were you in, which Revelation did you experience?* The early ones—Pakistan, Israel, Egypt—they get the most sympathy; they were the most brutal. I was so young, I barely remember those first few images that appeared on our TVs in late 2024. We've all seen those famous pictures so many times now, the Pakistani woman with her eyes bugging out, the heaps of bodies in the center of Islamabad. But at the age of eight, anything more than twenty minutes from my hometown of Tutelo, Virginia, might as well have been Antarctica.

I remember hovering around my mother as she and my father clicked frantically on their computers for the latest updates. It didn't seem any different to me than the usual horrors on the news—the wars, the famines—but my parents could tell it was. My mother kept telling me that everything would be okay, that we would be safe. But her words were far from comforting for one simple reason: I had never considered that we *wouldn't* be safe.

My father, a small-town minister (how archaic that term seems now), busied himself with work—writing his sermons, traveling to see other religious leaders. Unlike my friends from more secular homes, I'd lived with God as a reality since birth. When people began to whisper that we were entering a purge akin to the age of Noah's ark, I had my father to reassure me. He was working to save us all. He even told me that date, July 4, before anyone else knew. My father explained that Great Spirit (yes, there was no more God now, only Great Spirit) was smart. For the American Revelation, He knew to pick a day we'd remember.

So where was I on July 4, 2025? Where do you think I was? The same place you were, if you lived through that day and survived to read these words. We all knew it was coming—Prophet Joshua had been preaching about it for weeks. Every store was closed in preparation. Religious and political leaders had one common instruction; they'd found one common thread among those who had been spared in previous Revelations. They told us all to get to a worship center of some kind, to hunker down as though it were a shelter from the storm.

Maybe other families didn't have faith like mine did, but if you looked around our church that July 4 morning, you'd never have guessed that. It was packed to the brim, standing room only. I still remember the heat, the sweat of that room, the smell of all those anxious bodies packed together as we waited for our lives to change.

My mother sat next to me in the front row while my dad

spoke at the pulpit. She held my hand as I trembled. A little girl next to me was positively shaking with fear. She was a little older than me and wearing a white headscarf. Muslim, she would have called herself. But today, for the first time, the old religions didn't matter. In a moment, I knew, we would all be the same. It was my first inkling of the world to come.

We'd been in that room for hours and hours . . . an eternity for a child of nine, and I desperately had to pee. My mother told me to wait, to try to hold it for a break in the hymns, then finally relented and told me to go.

When I got back, my mom was gone. I looked all around, I paced up and down every row. A middle-aged blond woman told me my mother had gone to find me, that I should sit and wait, she'd be right back. I waited next to this stranger, growing more anxious as the clock ticked on. And then, while I was waiting—it happened. The Revelation.

Most of you experienced the Moment, but I know it was a little different for everyone. I've heard some compare it to the calm of deep meditation, to the catharsis of a spiritual release, but to me it felt like being lifted. I was sure I'd been physically lifted off the floor, though I was told my feet remained firmly planted on planet Earth. Everything around me shimmered, and the people around me *shone*. I'd never seen anything like it. All I knew was I was at peace, the world was at peace, and everything from then on would be okay. Still thinking in my old Christian vernacular, I was sure this was a glimpse of heaven, the beginning of paradise on earth. That experience is still more real to me, more visceral, than any that's come between to try to replace it.

"You are protected," my father intoned to all assembled. Each, I realized later, was on a spiritual journey similar to my own, lost in hazes of personal heaven. As every world religious leader had told us—at this moment, we would become something new. Adherents of the Universal Theology. Followers of a new, all-encompassing, all-powerful deity: Great Spirit.

Though none of us were Christian, or Jewish, or Muslim anymore, my father still quoted the Bible—all he knew at the time, all he knew most of us knew: "The Great Spirit of all religions Forgives you. In the words of Ecclesiastes 3:11: 'He has made everything beautiful in its time. He has put eternity into man's heart, so he cannot find out what God'"—he caught himself—"'Great Spirit, has done from the beginning to the end.'"

My father knew the question we'd all been asking ourselves since those first images emerged from Pakistan—we wanted to know just how we would fare in Great Spirit's Great Judgment. Ushers came down the aisles with mirrors—not nearly enough, since no one had expected a crowd this size, but we took turns—and when a mirror came to me, I was shocked. I had never seen myself healthier, more vibrant, more perfect. It wasn't that any of my features had changed shape, just that they somehow worked together better. I looked healthy. I glowed like the people around me. That was the first time I was conscious of what beauty was, and immediately I understood its power and importance. "You are the blameless ones," I heard my father say. "By coming here today, you have rid yourselves of sin and blame, and you have all been declared pious in the eyes of Great Spirit." One look around proved this to be true. Not a single person in that room had been Punished. Getting to my father's worship center had saved us all.

The high, that feeling of everlasting peace and contentment, continued for several days. But through that haze of bliss, one thing still concerned me—my mother's continued absence. My father explained that one of his junior clerics had intercepted her returning from the bathroom. She was urgently needed for a matter of great importance. She was running an errand on Great Spirit's behalf, but she'd be right back. The way he said it—that was my model, in later years, for what my father looks like when he lies to protect me.

Finally, nearly a week later, my father broke the news. I don't know how long he'd known, or whether he'd simply given up hope. My mother wasn't coming back.

"Is she dead?" I asked.

My father hates to be direct, hates to say things that scare him out loud. But for me, he had to try. He nodded, and my heart broke.

"What happened?"

"She's been in the hospital. She was very sick. The doctors did everything they could."

I was angry with my father for not taking me to see her, not giving me one final goodbye. But as I grew older, and he continued to evade my questions about her death, I thought of another possibility. Perhaps she hadn't been taken down by some mysterious calamity, coincidentally at the moment of the Revelation. The only logical explanation I could think of was the one I was afraid to imagine, the one my father would have been too ashamed to tell me. She must not have been Forgiven. She must have been purged, Punished, like so many in the weeks before her, and so many in the years to come.

Great Spirit had taken my mother from me. Years later He would take Jude from me. My father, the cleric, was at a loss to explain either. Weeks after Jude's crash, we found out that the woman who'd been driving the sedan, the mother of the child who died—that woman lived. She'd remain an Outcast for life, surely, but she had not been Punished as severely as Jude. Why? I asked my father. How could that be? He babbled platitudes about surrendering to Great Spirit's will, that we aren't meant to understand why He chooses to Punish who He does. But I saw through them. My father, too, was thrown. He, too, was confused. He, too, wanted answers.

Maybe if he'd found the right words, he could have eliminated that seed of doubt that had taken root in my mind. But no, I can't blame my father. However this story might turn out in later years, it began in the most banal, superficial of ways. I ended up where I ended up because I was a seventeen-year-old girl, and seventeen-year-old girls will always be weak when it comes to one thing: seventeen-year-old boys.

# CHAPTER 2

I don't know what dating was like in the pre-Revelation era. I'm sure looks were always important. But for the girls in my class, it was all we talked about. Did Aiden's dreamy eyes mean he was a better person than Devon, with his sexy biceps? The debates raged endlessly. There was Henry, who'd lived in Africa for a year tutoring orphans and had the most amazing six-pack. Thomas, who carried around a prayer mat and faced Mecca during the school day, and who had the most envied shiny blond surfer hair.

I don't know if the boys judged us with the same scrutiny. Jude was my only male friend, and he was too embarrassed to talk about that kind of thing with me. Sex was the one thing the prophets never really touched. For all the time they spent railing against murder and theft and unkindness, they always managed to avoid passing judgment on the one thing everyone my age wanted to know about. Sure, they advised against adultery, and Prophet Joshua made a strong statement in support of homosexuality, in contradiction to some of the more conservative prophets, but sex in general? You'd get a peep about personal choice, or you'd hear something from a prophet in Asia or Africa promoting abstinence before marriage. Prophet Navid was even in favor of polygamy. For the most part, the prophets said that all was Forgiven prior to Great Spirit bringing His heaven to earth, but to exercise caution in the future. That sex was about procreation and expressing love, a kind of vague monogamy-is-good stance.

And indeed, Great Spirit seemed inconsistent in His application of Punishment when it came to sex. In big cities, I'd heard that people lived similarly to the pre-Revelation era. More monogamy, more marriage, but plenty of cohabitation and hookups. But where I was from? In Virginia, I saw girls "go ugly," and over the next nine months you'd realize why. My dad had an easy explanation for this one—it had to do with love, with the virtuousness in your heart. If you entered a sexual encounter with the purest intentions, of staying with that person, of devoting yourself to him or her through thick and thin, then Great Spirit condoned your liaison. If the encounter was of a carnal nature, if it was selfish, if you thought of yourself and your own pleasure and not your partner's well-being, if you were using him or her in any way, then Great Spirit saw fit to Punish you in relation to the severity of your crime. My father said that's why the rate of Punishment among teenagers having sex was so high—we were more driven by our base instincts than adults, more likely to have sex for selfish, impure reasons than those older than us.

All this is to say—my friends and I were not having sex. It was too risky. How were you supposed to know if you were having sex in a truly devoted way? And what if your boyfriend wasn't? By giving in to intercourse, were you dooming him to life as an Outcast? Or worse, tying yourself to someone who was now less attractive? Because if he hadn't truly devoted himself to you, he'd become uglier. And then what? You couldn't break up with him, that would prove you weren't devoted, which meant you were stuck with this ugly sinner. It was complicated.

Of course I'd already analyzed all of this to death with my best girl friend, Macy. Macy got a lot of attention from guys. She was pretty, of course; I wouldn't have been friends with anyone who wasn't. But she was the one with personality. She had a biting wit, but she delivered her jabs softly, so you felt even as she teased you, that she really cared. In our friendship, I think I followed her lead on just about everything. When it came to Great Spirit, I had loads to say, but when it came to school, to anything in the social spheres, taste in music—I deferred to Macy. She had strong opinions, and I found it easier to echo hers than to formulate my own.

When it came to dating, Macy had the strongest opinions of all. I couldn't date Thomas, ugh, that prayer mat was so pretentious. I mean, it's nice that he's pious, and yes, she'd love to run her fingers through his hair, but really, has he washed that thing? She heard he used it to pray in the boys' bathroom, gross. And on and on. She was one of the ones who teased me about Jude while he was alive, but after he died, of course, she told me she always thought that we were soulmates. Great timing, thanks, Macy.

After Jude died, honestly, I wasn't interested in dating. Or eating. Or moving. I'd been through this once with my mother. For months after she died, it was like living life through a fog.

And in some ways, that fog never really lifted. The one thing that got me through that grief was Jude. He showed up at my door the day of her funeral, dressed in his little black suit, to give me his condolences—coaxed over by his parents, no doubt. But no one instructed him to sit with me day after day, no matter how sullen I was, no matter how un-fun to play with . . . until finally, months later, he convinced me to sit next to him in our imaginary rocket to Jupiter. And as we explored the stars, I started to experience joy again. Even at ten he had a compassionate heart—and once he was gone, I couldn't find another quite like it. Macy tried to understand my grief, all my friends did, but I could see their frustration mount when I said again that I wasn't in the mood to go out, or when I'd get distracted and space out at the lunch table. And as months and then years passed, I thought I would feel better, but I felt worse. I missed Jude's empathetic presence in my life, and that made me miss Jude himself even more. Every night in my dreams, I clung to that kind-eyed EMT, breathing in the sharp, floral scent of her perfume as I watched Jude roll away in that ambulance.

My dad, despite having no spiritual answers, had some pretty good secular ones to get me back on my feet. Like, "If you get out of bed and go to school, I'll burp the ABCs in the middle of my sermon on Sunday." And he did. It's still on YouTube; it's pretty funny.

I don't mean to make such a big deal of my grief. I know I'm not the first person to lose a friend, and I've lost many more since. We all have. I simply mean to set the stage for the fact that eventually, I got better. And it's when I got better that I met Ciaran.

# CHAPTER 3

As much as being pious helped your skin tone, no one could deny that Great Spirit had not stopped the aging process. And while plastic surgery had fallen out of fashion as both a selfish waste of money and a dishonest cheat, many other industries cropped up to take its place. More than ever before, middle-aged women spared no expense trying to regain their youth.

Macy's mother went to Haiti every year, part of a regular group doing charity work with orphans. My dad let me go with her once, and the missions on the ground were incredible. You'd see women, mostly from the U.S. and Canada, building a housing project like trained pros, yelling to each other over the sounds of chainsaws. They'd wear these big veils to protect themselves from the sun—no point going all that way just to get sun damage. Looking around that island, you'd think Haiti had been turned into an all-female penal colony.

Like Macy's mom, they'd arrive a little worn down, tired

from their jobs on the mainland. After a week of distributing water and teaching and prayer (nothing beautified you like prayer) they'd leave looking five, ten years younger. No one understood why I came. "You're so young," they said. "You don't need to be here. You're beautiful already."

That experience did not deter me. After that, I began volunteering regularly at a care home for Outcasts. These were people whose lifetime accumulation of Punishments kept them ostracized from mainstream society, and often incapacitated them. Many had difficulties breathing or walking, as their muscles had atrophied or seized. Often they couldn't get jobs and had been abandoned by their friends and families out of shame or necessity.

Quite a lot was misunderstood about Outcasts. They were seen as worse than homeless—they were assumed to be criminals, deviants, hopeless causes. My father thought differently—he had done quite a bit of outreach to their communities. While I didn't have my father's courage to go to every street corner and talk to strangers with mangled faces, I was inspired to do that work in a much safer environment. Care homes gave Outcasts much-needed medical attention, a community, and the kind of prayer they needed to maybe, possibly, get better.

I saw only one man fully heal while I volunteered there, a middle-aged former truck driver named Clint Ramsey. He had been an alcoholic prior to the Revelations, and he couldn't break the habit once Great Spirit commanded moderation. He'd destroyed his relationships with his wife and teenage son, and a series of small sins slowly eroded his physical body. Clint confided that his wife, Rowena, had filed for divorce after Clint, in a drunken stupor, had verbally accosted their son. Near the end, Clint couldn't walk, and luckily, he couldn't lift a bottle to take a drink. So he found his way to the Harrisonburg Care Center. The women there prayed with him, they made him feel safe, they told him how Great Spirit Forgives. And little by little, Great Spirit Forgave Clint. By the time I arrived, six months into his rehabilitation, he already looked like a person again. He probably could have gone out into the real world, but he wasn't ready. He wanted to stay and heal as much as he could before exposing himself to the temptations of the outside world.

By the time he was leaving, not that I was interested in fifty-year-old men, I had to admit that Clint was quite the looker. All the single women in the center were head over heels, but he was single-minded. He wanted to reconcile with his wife.

Rowena had come to the center a few times during the year Clint was there. He was hopeful, he told me, because she still hadn't filed the divorce papers. He believed that in spite of everything—and I could tell from his tone that "everything" was something much darker than he was willing to admit—he believed she still loved him. I was there the day he was released, and she came to pick him up. It was just Clint and me sitting at a table in the common room when Rowena Ramsey walked in. I'd never seen a picture, but I knew immediately who she was. She was pretty despite her frown lines, in her forties, a powerful presence. She looked at me with sharp, untrusting eyes, and I was wise enough to skedaddle when I saw her coming. I wished Clint my best and slipped out the door—and in doing so, bumped into a tall, dark figure—a handsome seventeen-year-old boy.

"I'm so sorry," I said, startled. It was mostly older women who worked at the care center. Rarely did I see a non-Outcast my own age there, and never one as good-looking as him.

He didn't respond as I expected—most people apologize profusely for any possible trespass, afraid of offending Great Spirit. But he just looked at me with his deep blue eyes. He resembled Clint enough that the first words out of his mouth didn't surprise me. "You know my dad?"

I nodded. "Clint? I've been working with him for a while." I peeked into the common room—Rowena and Clint were deeply engaged in conversation. I turned back to their son, who had gone quiet. I chimed in again, hoping to engage him. "Your father speaks very highly of you. He regrets the mistakes he's made."

"What kind of mistakes did he tell you about?"

The boy watched me closely. I knew quite a bit about this stranger's private life, which I worried might make him uncomfortable. "Oh, just sort of in general, that he was sorry."

His voice held a challenge. "So now that you're the expert on my family—you think my parents are gonna get back together?"

I didn't know a lot about divorced people, so I answered the question I did have a depth of knowledge in. "Your father's developed a really beautiful relationship with Great Spirit."

He seemed amused by that. Many things, I noticed, seemed to amuse him. "Guess that can't hurt," was all he said.

"It must be hard for you, all this stuff with your parents," I said, trying to prove how compassionate I could be.

"I guess. You talk to them more than I do. Why do you come here?"

This launched me into a long spiel—that the most important thing you can do in life is to cultivate a relationship with Great Spirit, and to help others do the same. "You have to do as much as you can, because you never know how much will be enough, and the difference between success and failure . . . that's someone's life."

"Who did you fail?" It was like he'd read my mind.

"Why do you assume that?"

He shrugged. "I don't know."

I found the words tumbling out of me. "I lost a friend."

"What happened to her?"

"*He* caused a car crash. Two years ago. Great Spirit didn't Forgive him."

"That sucks." He must have seen he'd hit a nerve, and changed the subject. "You live around here?"

I told him I went to school about an hour away. That my father was the cleric of Tutelo Valley Worship Center, formerly the Tutelo Presbyterian Church, if he'd heard of it?

"Cleric's daughter, huh?" For some reason, his smirking smile gave me butterflies.

"You should come to services sometime. Though I'm sure you already have a worship center." I gestured to him sort of stupidly. Great, I'd just told him he was hot. The little I knew about the mating game told me that was a terrible move.

But he just laughed. "I'll try."

At that moment, Rowena Ramsey came out. Gave me that same suspicious glare. "Ciaran! Let's go."

She looked at him expectantly. He ignored her. "What was your name again?"

"Grace."

He gave me a wink as he headed off after his mother. "See you around, cleric's daughter."

# CHAPTER 4

Of course, after an interaction of that magnitude with a boy of that level of hotness, I immediately downloaded with Macy. We sat in her living room snacking on veggies and hummus, dissecting every moment, every pause. I worried that he didn't like that I was a cleric's daughter.

"Grace. Everyone likes that you're a cleric's daughter." I started to protest, but Macy cut me off. "Seriously. You should hear people talk."

"Why?" I wondered.

"Because it means you're hot. Because it means you'll be hot your whole life, even after you get married. And it makes you different. Why do you think everyone likes Weird Prayer Mat Thomas?"

"You hate Weird Prayer Mat Thomas!"

"But he's had two girlfriends. Devon's way hotter, and he hasn't had any."

We spent the next several minutes debating whether Weird

Prayer Mat Thomas's two girlfriends were really all that pretty, and whether Devon could have gotten them to go out with him if he'd asked, and Devon doesn't ask anyone out so it isn't really a fair comparison. We both agreed we'd go out with Devon if he asked us, but that maybe he was gay, because why else would he let all that go to waste?

Finally, we turned to the much more important topic of Ciaran, and we again agreed that it was cool that he went to another school because it gave him an air of mystery, and I could avoid being the subject of gossip if it didn't work out.

"But what if I never see him again?" The thought had only now crossed my mind.

"You know his dad, don't you?"

"I'm not going to ask his dad for his number. Plus, his dad's leaving the center."

"So go back tomorrow. Maybe he'll still be there."

But I was already despairing. "Why didn't I get his number?"

"Why didn't he get your number, that's the question. It's not your job to get his number." Macy couldn't help but add, "Or you could always date his dad, right? You said he's a hottie?"

I rolled my eyes. "Yeah, I love old dudes."

Of course, that was the moment Macy's brother, Zack, chose to enter the room. Zack wasn't really an old dude, but he was twenty-two, a full five years and a whole statutory rape Punishment older than me. I didn't know Zack well—he was a real grown-up who worked in D.C. He only came home every once in a while for business and mostly kept to himself. I got the sense that there was a lot more to him than I saw—that as his little sister's friend, I mattered so little that I didn't get to witness the full Zack experience. Which, of course, only made me want to see it more. I don't want to say that I had a crush on him . . . he was far too old for that. And if Macy was going to tease me for having a crush on Prayer Mat Thomas, it would have been the end of our friendship if I admitted to liking her brother.

All that said . . . when he walked into the room and overheard me, I blushed.

"Don't mind me," he said, grabbing a handful of celery sticks.

"Hey! Make your own snacks," Macy snapped.

Zack smiled. "I'm a guest here now."

"So is Grace, and these snacks are for her."

Zack turned to me, and I stammered, "I'm staying out of this."

Macy said, "See, you're making Grace uncomfortable."

"By taking celery sticks?"

"Mom says you have to be nicer to me, buttloser."

"Mom says you're going to get yourself Punished if you keep calling me buttloser."

"Great Spirit already knows you're a buttloser."

"Great Spirit thinks I'm awesome." Zack gestured to his face and body, and I had to admit, he had a point.

"Great Spirit really loves your humility."

They continued their sibling rivalry into the kitchen. I rose to follow, but just as I approached the door, Zack turned so suddenly, I almost smacked into him. I blushed. Again. For some reason, I was very prone to blushing around Zack.

"Macy's making more snacks," he said.

"That's nice of her."

"Not really. I gave her ten bucks. That's the beauty of being a grown-up. You make money to pay servants."

"Oh."

"So who's this guy?"

Had he overheard our conversation? "What guy?"

"Macy says you have the hots for some guy."

I played dumb. "I don't know what you're talking about."

"He's got a girl's name, right? Karen?"

"Ciaran. I worked with his dad, at a care center."

"Ah." It took Zack a moment to process that. "You shouldn't date that kid."

"Why?" I asked.

Zack didn't come back with an easy answer. "His dad's in a care center. That's not good. That's not the kind of guy you should date."

"He's no sinner."

"You never know. Boys like that, they're not always what they seem. Trust me—I'm older; I've seen it. Guys like that are trouble."

At this point, I was just annoyed. "You've never even met him."

"I don't need to."

"Why do you care who I date?"

"If you start dating him, you'll introduce my sister to one of his friends. I don't want to have to go beat up some hick future Outcast when he treats my sister badly, and then get Punished for it."

"You've thought this out."

Zack remained totally serious. "I like to think ahead. Nip the problem in the bud here and now."

"That's very thoughtful of you."

"Big brother's gotta do what a big brother's gotta do."

Zack gave me one more pointed look as I sat processing what he'd just said. As frustrated as I was that Zack was trying to dictate my dating habits without professing any interest in dating me himself, I knew the chances I'd see Ciaran again were small. What did it matter anyway? Looking back, I can't help but wish I'd taken Zack's advice.

# CHAPTER 5

I did take Macy's suggestion to go back to the center, but Clint had already checked out. No one knew where to, though they'd heard not to Rowena's house, which left the single volunteers some hope. I didn't want to ask about Ciaran. Macy was right—if he hadn't liked me enough to ask me out, that was that.

Several uneventful weeks passed, and we found other things to talk about. Did Devon just look at Aiden in, like, a sexy way? Maybe they're both gay and not acting on it because they fear Great Spirit's wrath? Ugh, then there would be no cute guys in our school.

There was, however, one moment worth mentioning. I know I said I would never have been friends with anyone who wasn't pretty, and I wish I could say that was an exaggeration—I certainly was raised to be more tolerant and welcoming. My father, in his work with Outcasts, would often talk about how they were no different from him and me—a combination of circumstances or a bad choice could doom someone to a completely different path. My experience with Jude should have helped me to realize just how true that was—instead, I grew more and more wary of those whose faces hinted at a history of ungodly behavior.

There weren't many Outcasts at my school. There were many more in cities than suburbs like Tutelo, and most Outcast kids dropped out of school as soon as they could. But there was one girl, Ann, who had once been bright and beautiful and normal. I don't know what her Punishment was for—Outcasts generally kept that to themselves—but sometime during sophomore year, after a long absence, she returned to school with a terrifying face that no one in my social circle would go near.

She still did well in school, and she was applying to college—a rarity for Outcast teens. She was the only Outcast in my AP World History class, and she sat in the back, with her sickly, stringy hair and terrible breath, avoiding the rest of us. I was still morose about my missed opportunity with Ciaran, so when our teacher partnered me for a project with Ann, I didn't take it well. Ann was nice enough during our planning session, as we talked about various multimedia options for relaying the biography of our assigned prophet, Japan's Hashimoto. But when I got to gym class and had a moment alone with Macy, I couldn't resist mocking the raspy way Ann spoke. "How stupid will we sound talking about Hashimoto?" I did a long, detailed impression of Ann's "speech," and it wasn't until the bell rang and we walked out of the locker room that I noticed a small figure sitting alone, one aisle over from where Macy and I had been talking. Ann, clearly within earshot, not even willing to look at me.

A glance in the mirror told me I was getting a slight Punishment for my actions—a little asymmetry in my face, some thinning of my wild curls, but that wasn't the end of it. Our teacher pulled me aside after class. "Ann says she needs to change teammates."

I explained, and apologized, but she wasn't having it. "What about your friend Jude? Would you have said those things to him?"

I thought it was low of her to bring up Jude. "No," I said, "I wouldn't have."

"Ann's going to have it hard enough in life. Don't go making it worse. You're better than this. You're one of the good ones."

One of the good ones. How little I'd done to deserve that praise. I did apologize to Ann, who gratefully accepted. All was Forgiven, for me at least, and we did our project together. Her raspy voice said plenty of intelligent things about Hashimoto, and for the next week I offered to let Ann sit at our lunch table. I hoped, perhaps, Great Spirit might reward me for my kindness to this Outcast girl. And then one day, He did.

Every Sunday since that fateful care center meeting, I'd kept an eye out for Ciaran. I didn't think he'd really drive an hour just to see me. But it was the one way he knew to find me, and in my most hopeful fantasies, I would turn around during my father's sermon and see him sitting behind me, smiling that sexy half smile. But in real life, real Sunday after real Sunday, there was no sign of him. I started to feel stupid. What had really gone on between us? He'd asked me some questions about his dad. He'd winked at me, for fun, as he left. Nothing more.

But then, as I walked up the steps of our worship center one chilly Sunday morning, I saw him. Sitting on a bench outside the front doors, wrapped up in a big woolen parka, eyes fixed on his phone. I couldn't believe it.

"Ciaran?" He glanced up. There was that dazzling smile.

My father gave me a knowing look. "I'll see you inside." My father often gave sermons about the difficulties of raising children in the post-Revelation era, but in this one instance, I think he must have had it easier. One glance at Ciaran's perfectly symmetrical bone structure and my father knew I'd found a trustworthy young man.

As my dad disappeared into the church, I sat down next to Ciaran. "What are you doing here?" I asked him.

"Thought I'd come see your dad in action."

"Ah," I said, with my usual eloquence under pressure.

"He's related to you. He's gotta be cool, for a cleric." He put a hand on the small of my back, and an excited shiver went down my spine. "Shall we?"

## CHAPTER 6

When the service was over, we wandered around the worship center grounds. I asked what school he went to, and he was evasive. "I've been to a couple."

"Because your family moved?"

"Just 'cause."

"Where do you go now?"

I still don't know why he didn't answer that question. Maybe he wanted to keep an air of mystery. Maybe he thought the truth would scare me off. In any case, he maneuvered the topic around to what he'd been trying to ask me all day. "What are you doing tomorrow night?"

"Monday? A school night?"

"You aren't gonna spend the whole night studying, are you?"

"But my father and I have game night on Mondays" sounded unbearably lame, so I didn't say that. I said, "Of course not."

"Then come out with me."

"Where?"

"Does it matter?"

I tried to pretend like it did. "Of course."

"There's something I want to show you."

"What?"

He hesitated. "Eh, you're not ready."

"Not ready for what?" He just smiled coyly. Let me spin for a minute. "What?" I begged.

"It's a secret."

"Now you have to tell me!"

"It's *my* secret," he said.

"That's not an answer," I pointed out. "What kind of secret is it? A bad secret?"

"Of course it's not a bad secret."

"Then why aren't you telling me?"

"You're not ready."

I was getting frustrated. "What are you talking about? What do I have to do to be ready?" He looked me up and down, weighing his options.

"Come out with me tomorrow night, and I'll tell you."

I had no reason to say no. Great Spirit had made no commandments that teens couldn't go out on school nights. Here was a good, pious young man, making a statement I could tell was true by looking at his unchanging face. My father would be overjoyed that after years of staying in my room in a Jude-related depression, I'd made plans with a new friend. But something held me back. Did I feel guilty about Jude? In retrospect, I can say for certain, not one iota. Was I afraid to fall for someone new, after such a traumatic loss? Maybe. Perhaps it was some kind of intuition I'd never needed to use before. All I know is, when Ciaran spoke, something in me wanted to flee, and I had no explanation for why. But of course, the only thing I was ever going to say was "Sure."

Ciaran smiled. He really did have an amazing smile.

# CHAPTER 7

My father had exactly the reaction I'd anticipated. He knew how hard I had taken Jude's death these past two years, so when I told him about the date with Ciaran, he said, "That's wonderful! I have a meeting in D.C. that night, so I won't be back until early in the morning. You'll be okay letting yourself in?"

Okay, now all of you who were teenagers pre-Revelation are freaking out. But that's just how it was. We didn't have strict guidelines or curfews because Great Spirit provided them for us. Parents could look at you and know you weren't lying about your plans, and wherever you went, Great Spirit's laws kept you safe from anyone who might want to harm you.

So my father left for his meeting. My makeup was done, my outfit was stressed about. Macy had given her blessing to our union, as well as her word that she wouldn't be waiting in the bushes, watching to see how hot he was.

When Ciaran finally did arrive, I couldn't believe how nervous I was. With Jude, I'd known him so long that we were already comfortable by the time I bothered to develop a crush. With Ciaran . . . this was the first real date I'd ever been on, and everything was unknown. The wrong word or gesture could scare him away.

"So?" I asked before my feet had even crossed the threshold to leave the house.

"So what?"

"Secret, *por favor?*" I extended my hand, as though expecting him to pass it to me. He grinned, pleased I'd remembered.

"Oh, you'll find out. But first . . ." He took my hand and wrapped it around his arm, like we were an old-timey lady and gentleman. "We have quite a night ahead of us."

First on the itinerary was a movie. I was quite impressed when he led me in the side entrance. It turned out he had a cousin who owned the theater, and he was able to see movies for free, whenever he wanted, with whomever he wanted. So after two hours of your standard boy meets girl, boy encounters the forces of evil, boy glorifies Great Spirit and gets the girl story, we headed out in search of sustenance.

"Do you want some ice cream or something?"

I wanted to say yes, because it's hard to say anything but yes to someone so cute, but even with thick tights, my much stressed about date dress was not appropriate for the chilly winds blowing around us. I blurted out, "In this weather?"

He registered my shivering and made a second offer. "Do you want my coat?" Then, perhaps not wanting to be cold himself, he saw an open clothing store and said, "I have a better idea." He whisked me inside and gestured to the store's offerings. "Take your pick."

I looked in my purse, the tiny one I'd chosen for the occasion. "I didn't bring enough money."

"My treat," he dismissed. He picked up a black hoodie. "Do you like this?"

"I couldn't."

"Of course you could. Pick one out." No boy had ever even bought me dinner before—a coat seemed extravagant. I had an inkling of what the price tags in this store might say. But if he was movie theater royalty . . .

"This one." He took the cute red jacket I handed him and glanced at the cashier, who was helping another customer. And then he put the jacket under his coat.

It took me a moment to register what was happening. By the time I realized he was leaving without paying for it, like the rebellious teenagers in pre-Revelation movies, I was left with no choice but to trail after him like a confused, nervous puppy.

"What are you doing?" I hissed as we stepped onto the sidewalk.

"Keep walking."

I kept a steady clip behind him. "That was wrong. You have to go give it back, or—"

"Or what?" It dawned on me that he remained unchanged. Face unblemished, muscles with their full vitality.

I tried to make sense of it. "Great Spirit's going to notice any minute. Go give that back."

"Great Spirit already did notice. He doesn't care."

My tone became more urgent. "Yes, He does."

"Not about me. You wanted to know my secret, didn't you? This is it. I'm special."

"Special how?"

"I'm blessed by Great Spirit." I looked at him. He didn't seem any different from any of the other kids I knew.

"How do you know?"

"My whole life, when other kids disobeyed their parents and saw Great Spirit's wrath? I never did. There's nothing I can do that will make Great Spirit harm me."

He wrapped the new red jacket around my shoulders. I let him. "Is that better?"

"I'm warmer."

"Don't be scared, Grace."

"Why haven't I heard about people like you before?"

"You think your father's gonna go up and tell everyone that no matter how hard they work, no matter what they do, Great Spirit will never love them like He loves me? That Great Spirit kills people like your friend, but I'll always be Forgiven?"

"Don't talk about Jude like that."

"That's his name? Jude? Were you in love with him or something?"

"He was my best friend."

"Oh." After a bit, Ciaran offered, "Being depressed about it won't bring him back."

My mind was spinning. I had so many questions. "How many people like you are there?"

"I don't know. I've never met anyone else like me. I guess I could be the only one."

"Why do you think Great Spirit picked you?"

"I don't know."

"You think you're meant for something special?"

"I know I am."

"Like what?"

"Hang around, maybe you'll find out."

I was still shivering. And I was still a little mad about the coat thing. Stubbornly, I pouted. "No."

He took my hands, warmed them in his. Soft. Tender. He whispered, "If you stay with me, Great Spirit will protect you, too."

I couldn't believe that. "How will Great Spirit protect me?"

"The same way He protects me. I don't know." I could tell he was getting annoyed by all my questions. "What was it your father said in his sermon about surrendering to Great Spirit's will?"

"So you're a cleric now?"

He shrugged. "I don't know anything . . . I just know you're really beautiful."

Beautiful. He let go of my hands and took hold of the empty sleeves of my new jacket, using them to pull me close. There were butterflies in my stomach now. It felt too good to be true—that someone Great Spirit had chosen would really select me, out of all the girls in the world. I asked, "Why me?"

He seemed taken aback by the question. "Why you? Because I think you're special, too."

He put a hand to my face and then—it happened. He kissed me. There it was, my first kiss. As magical as I'd always imagined. More magical, because the boy I was with was more magical than anyone I'd ever imagined.

Driving back from the movie, I noticed Ciaran wasn't wearing a seat belt. He didn't have to, I realized. He was in no danger. From anything. I tried to keep that in mind as he sped down the dark, winding roads.

"So am I taking you home?"

It was 11 P.M. As someone who'd been in bed early every night before this one, who rarely went to events unrelated to our worship center or volunteer work, the world suddenly felt much wider. "Where else would you take me?"

"I have a couple ideas. What would you want to do?"

"Anything." I paused. "Something I've never done before."

"Something you could only do with me?"

"Yeah."

"Somewhere you've never even heard of?"

My heart raced with the thrill. "Absolutely."

"Hold on, cleric's daughter." He pulled a terrifyingly unsafe U-turn, and we were off.

# CHAPTER 8

I t was certainly somewhere I'd never heard of. I told you about my time at the care center helping to rehabilitate Outcasts, so I wasn't revolted by them like so many of my peers. And I knew there were millions, so there couldn't have been care centers enough to hold them all, especially not the poorest ones. Still, I had always imagined Outcasts as mole people, living in makeshift huts in alleyways, shuffling through the streets of big cities under the cover of night.

In reality, the Outcasts had quite a vibrant society. I'd soon be exposed to it plenty more, but my first encounter was with Ciaran, on the night of our first date. We parked on an empty street crawling with cockroaches—the kind of place that might have made me nervous, had we still lived in a crime-filled world.

As I opened my door to get out, I saw a man approaching. Instinctively, I smiled, friendly . . . but as he stepped into the light, I saw his face was twisted, and he was limping. Most shockingly, there was a tube sticking out of his throat, like the ones given to emphysema patients after a tracheotomy, making an earthy rattling sound. He needed it to breathe, I realized, to keep from being choked to death from the inside, like Jude was.

The man got into his car, and I moved to walk closer to Ciaran. "Where are we?"

"Right now, we're on the street." He had discovered that answering my questions literally was the easiest way to annoy me.

"Right. Well, where are we going?"

He pointed to a building—no sign on the wall. "We're going shopping."

"In that old abandoned building?"

But as we approached I heard a hum of activity inside. Voices. Excitement. Ciaran held the door open for me. "Welcome to the black market."

# CHAPTER 9

The post-Revelation age was a world devoid of its previous sadness. Budgets once spent on armies were now spent on healthcare and emergency response. Police departments were shells of their former selves—Great Spirit was police enough, and crime was almost nonexistent. Markets were stable, as people gave up economic excess in exchange for pious moderation and hard work. The tide was even turning on global warming, as every nation united to fund efficient public transit and alternative fuel research. Tragedies were few and far between, and rarely man-made.

But just a decade earlier, when I was a child? Tragedies were common. Wars were common. People lived in fear because you never knew if that stranger approaching you in the dark of night was good or evil. People watched the news because what happened in the world might affect their safety, their economic well-being. Stock markets worldwide were constantly going up and down, with all the cataclysms of war and corruption and doubt and debt, and people were constantly losing money.

But that chaos was nothing compared to 2024, when the Revelations first began. The world had seen recessions before, panic and rioting even, but this was unprecedented. People thought the world was ending, and their fear sent the already fragile economy tanking. And then Great Spirit started making Prohibitions. That was the biggest surprise, especially in Western countries where people were used to certain freedoms. Great Spirit, through His prophets, commanded moderation—no more binge drinking, and harsh Punishments for those using illegal drugs. He said they were interfering with our spiritual experience of His world. And, as my good friend Clint can tell you, Great Spirit made good on His promise to Punish all who disobeyed this law. But that wasn't the end of it—Great Spirit also warned merchants that they were responsible for the actions of those they sold to, meaning your local grocer got the same Punishment you did when you smoked the pack of cigarettes you bought from him. So almost overnight, out of self-preservation, stores stopped carrying potentially harmful goods. Which meant that in the past decade, I'd never seen any adult smoke a cigarette or have a drink.

I knew the Clints of the world must have found some way to access the drugs they remained addicted to. I don't know how manufacturers survived the process of selling them, but somehow fresh drugs kept making it into the general population. I'd just never considered where one might go to get them, until Ciaran walked me through those doors. The black market—that was a level of sophistication I'd never expected.

We arrived at midnight, and the place was still bustling. Everything smelled pungent and unfamiliar. Voices shouted over each other, haggling about prices, as I stood on tiptoes to see the merchandise over the shoulders of the crowd. Here was every item I knew Great Spirit Prohibited, and even more I'd never have thought of. Cigars, porn, tattoos. I saw a girl with her jaw loosely attached getting her hair cut in a colorful punk chop. I saw a couple with hands in each other's back pockets, their skin grimy and nearly falling off, heading out with a bag full of sex toys. The sounds of vigorous bartering encircled us. Everyone seemed to know everyone else, and they spoke in a shorthand I had trouble following.

Everywhere we walked, we got odd glances—we didn't belong. Every other person in here was an Outcast. Any store we walked up to, customers would quietly shuffle away, worried perhaps that we were part of some kind of god squad, coming to clean them up. Ciaran seemed to enjoy this status, and he enjoyed my awe even more.

"How do you know about this place?" I asked.

"Everyone does. I just knew you wouldn't."

"Because I'm sheltered?"

"Yeah."

I looked around. There wasn't anything here I could imagine wanting. It was like growing up in a land of gourmet food, then coming to a market full of rotten dog meat—we rarely want more than our culture has prescribed for us. And I was never an outside-the-box thinker, anyway. I preferred my life the way it always had been—safe, familiar. Except . . .

"What are these?" We'd approached a stand of movies, ones I'd never seen before.

"Movies. We just saw one earlier tonight, remember?"

"I've never heard of these ones."

"Really? These aren't even that bad." He seemed surprised, as though I was sheltered to a level he hadn't even considered. "This one's funny."

He handed me a comedy—the stars I recognized, the content I didn't. I thought I'd seen all the old movies there were. All they seemed to stream on TV were old movies. But then again . . . all they streamed on TV were things deemed "safe" in this new world. Of course there must have been movies from the twentieth century with content deemed offensive—too many swear words, too much violence. The racks of movies in front of me suggested that there were quite a few.

"Should I buy it?" I was feeling rebellious. All-powerful. Nothing could stop me, except that nagging doubt that . . . I shouldn't. That guilt, that worry that Great Spirit would Punish me. But He couldn't, could He? Wasn't I safe with Ciaran? But something felt off. I had a sick feeling in my stomach. Could Great Spirit be Punishing me right this moment?

My fears were confirmed when Ciaran took the movie from my hand, looking at me closely. "Don't buy it."

"Why? Do I look different?"

"Yeah, you're getting all gooey-eyed, it's embarrassing. Let's get out of here before people start looking at you funny."

"People have been looking at me funny since we walked in."

"Don't make it worse. You can't trust these people."

He whisked me away quickly. There were no mirrors anywhere inside the black market, for obvious reasons. When we reached the car, I glanced in the rearview mirror. My image, thankfully, had returned to normal. But I had an inkling that had I purchased that film, Ciaran's "blessing" would not have extended to me. I was no more immune from Great Spirit's Punishments than before.

And as we drove away from the black market, I no longer felt safe as Ciaran rounded turns blindly; even with my seat belt on, I jerked from side to side. Ciaran knew what life was like for someone blessed, but he had no idea how to protect someone who wasn't.

# CHAPTER 10

Somewhere around Ciaran's third speeding blind turn, I noticed that in addition to my wallet, I'd forgotten my phone at home. I'd been so engrossed in Ciaran, I'd given no thought to what Macy or my other friends might be texting me. But now, when I was starting to feel a little trapped, I regretted having nothing but a key, twenty dollars, and strawberry lip gloss in that tiny purse.

"I think I should be getting home."

"And why is that?" Ciaran leaned over to kiss me.

"Can you watch the road, please?" He pulled away, surprised by my sudden anxiety.

"Bossy. I like that."

"It's getting late. I have school in the morning."

"There's just one more thing I want to show you."

I remained silent. I didn't want to go. As much as I liked Ciaran and was in awe of the world he'd opened my eyes to, I was tired. I wanted to be at home, in bed, and I wanted time to process everything that had just happened. I didn't want to be forced to go to some strip club or some sin factory, or whatever else he thought might shock the sheltered cleric's daughter.

Ciaran was annoyed by my silence. "Okay?"

An older, less passive version of me would have said, *I said I wanted to go home, so please take me home.* Seventeen-year-old Grace said, grudgingly, "Okay."

We drove on in silence for a bit, and he put on some heavy metal. I was sure it was illegal, sinful music, which made me angrier with him. I couldn't understand why this kid was blessed, why Great Spirit would choose him over me. There was no one more pious than me, no one more dutiful. I knew Ciaran's lack of obedience must have come from a lifetime without Punishment, without fear, but I couldn't imagine that Great Spirit was really okay with that. The same nagging questions that had plagued me since Jude's death rose up again. I lived in a world that everyone agreed was just, but so many things still felt so unfair.

"We're here."

We didn't seem to be anywhere. We'd pulled off to the side of the road. To one side was a deep thicket of trees, black and menacing in the dark of night, and to the other was a clearing. Ciaran pulled out a blanket. "Have you ever seen the stars from this far out? Away from all the light pollution?"

Our worship center had sponsored many stargazing trips, so this was nothing special for me, but I was just so relieved he'd picked a Great Spirit–approved activity. "We're going stargazing?"

"That's right." He kissed me again. One by one, my worries, my spiritual anxieties melted away. This was all part of

Great Spirit's plan. Suddenly, this night could not have felt more perfect.

We lay on the blankets, cuddled up together for warmth, pointing out constellations. Good student that I was, I remembered all kinds of obscure ones. I knew all the zodiac signs, since every Sunday school studied a bit of astrology. Somewhere around Virgo, we got distracted, kissing. I couldn't believe it had been mere hours since he'd picked me up, when I'd been so nervous that he might not like me.

"You're special," he told me. "You know that, right?" I didn't. I wasn't, I can tell you in hindsight.

"I'm not special," I insisted. "You're the one with special powers. You're the one Great Spirit picked."

"And you're the only one I've ever told."

"Really?"

"Really."

"Why me?"

"I told you. I just sensed something about you. You're . . ."

"Special."

"Yeah." Even in that moment I didn't buy it. I barely knew him. Why would he have put me above every other friend and relative he'd ever met? But I was used to people telling the truth, and even though I knew his face wouldn't change if he lied, I wanted so badly to believe him, I didn't think too hard about what he was saying.

Things started to get more heated. He kissed my neck, so hard I was sure it must be bruising. His hands drifted down, grabbing my waist. As he unzipped my new red coat, I sat up.

"I think I should go home."

"Just a little bit longer."

He was pressing me to the ground, roughly. It was then it occurred to me that we were miles from anyone, anywhere. No cars had passed by.

"I want to go home."

"I'll take you home, don't worry." His hand had found its way under my skirt, stroking my thigh. This felt wrong, very wrong. I hadn't given a thought to what someone like Ciaran might want to do on a date with someone like me, but now it was painfully obvious.

"Ciaran . . ." I protested, but he put a finger to my lips. He was bigger than me. Stronger than me.

"Relax. Great Spirit wants this for you," he said.

"No," I said. He was unzipping his pants, it was all happening so fast. I tried to pray, but I realized I would get no help from Great Spirit now. Great Spirit had chosen Ciaran over me. Maybe Ciaran was right. Maybe this was His plan, my destiny. Maybe this is all I was ever supposed to be—someone like this to someone like Ciaran.

But no—I didn't want to worship anyone who would want this for me. For the first time, I asked myself what *I* wanted. Somewhere deep down, I found a power, an instinct I didn't even know was there. For a moment, my right leg was free, and I found a way to connect my knee with Ciaran's nose. It surprised him enough that he stood up, stepped back, and I ran, heels in my hands, across the empty road into the woods.

The soles of my feet stung with the sharpness of the forest

floor; my tights hung on my legs in shreds after only a few steps. But I ran, farther and farther, as far as I could go, holding my arms in front of me to avoid smashing into the trees I couldn't see.

After a moment, I paused, ducked behind a tree, listened to the stillness. I dared not move yet. I sat, waited. It felt like hours, but it must have been only ten or twenty freezing minutes. Every time a branch cracked, my heart skipped a beat, sure Ciaran was right behind me. The nighttime sounds of chirping crickets never seemed so cacophonous, so overwhelming.

I was nearly ready to venture back out, try to find my way home, when I heard it—a crackling of branches in a steady cadence. Step-step-step-step—a decidedly human sound. I stayed absolutely still. It was Ciaran, it had to be. But the forest was too large. He'd have to spend the night combing every tree to find my hiding place. As long as I made no sound, I'd give him no help.

But he seemed intent on finding me. His steady march continued, grew louder, softer, louder, softer, as he searched the woods near and far. . . . I couldn't bear it any longer. I had to peek, I had to see where he was. I saw a Ciaran-sized figure approaching in the distance. Headed my way.

I had two options. I could run, hoping to take advantage of my head start. But barefoot, I had no chance. I looked around for something to arm myself with. I'd fought him off last time, perhaps I could hold my own again. As quietly as I could, I picked up a nearby stick. If he found me, I was as ready as I could be.

The footsteps grew louder, closer. And in my peripheral vision, I saw him, wandering blindly through the forest. Heading deeper in, without seeing me. I was almost ready to breathe a sigh of relief. He would keep going, I thought, and I could run back out to the road, I could steal his truck and drive home, I could get to safety. The plan was so vivid it felt like it had already been accomplished.

Ciaran paused, his back to me. If he could pick out my hiding place, I'd be found. And I didn't know what would come next.

He waited there a long time. I couldn't tell if he'd spotted me, but I dared not breathe.

I'll never know if he did see me. Because the next thing I heard was the last thing I would have expected in that moment. It was loud, and it took me a moment to recognize it. A sound I'd never heard in person before, but must have heard in a movie as a small child because it had an echoing familiarity. Later, I'd call the sound a gunshot. Ciaran cried out, and then fell. I wanted to run over, find out what had happened, but I knew not to.

A second figure approached Ciaran's body. I don't know how the man was moving that soundlessly, but there he was, crouched over Ciaran. Confirming he was dead? I stared in horror at their silhouettes, trying to make sense of the scene in the dark. I was confused—it all felt surreal, but I knew that whatever danger Ciaran had posed to me, this mysterious figure could be a much greater threat. While the man's back was to me, I silently moved to the other side of the tree. Out of sight. But I was too curious not to peek out, to watch as he pulled out a phone and started typing. Illuminated by the light of the screen, the man's face was disgusting, marred by Outcast-level disfigurement. Had I wandered into some Outcast encampment? Did they shoot trespassers? How many more might be out there?

But then I saw the shooter pull out a small pill bottle, open it, and pour something into his hand. He swallowed it, no water. Instantly, his face transformed, regaining its healthy complexion, its symmetrical nature. And as it did, my stomach convulsed with panic. I recognized that face. It was one I'd seen many times.

The shooter was Macy's brother, Zack.

# BOOK
## TWO

# CHAPTER 1

I tried to process what I'd just seen. My best friend's brother, murdering my would-be date rapist. And craziest of all, that Zack had some kind of pill to counteract Great Spirit's Punishment for his crime. It all defied any sense of reason. Had some devil-like power seized control from Great Spirit, and mankind hadn't been informed?

And more importantly—did Zack know I was here? If he'd followed Ciaran into the woods, wouldn't he have known Ciaran was following me? Zack looked around, but his eyes never paused on me. Instead, he slung an unmoving Ciaran over his shoulder with ease. I'd never realized how strong Zack was. My mind spun. What possible connection could these two people have had to each other? When Zack warned me against dating Ciaran, was he already planning his murder?

As the sound of Zack's footsteps faded, I couldn't imagine ever moving from that spot. How was I supposed to go back to school, face my friends or my father, after witnessing that scene?

But as the wind grew colder on my bare and bloodied feet, I knew I couldn't stay in the woods. I began a countdown in my head, a number of seconds I was sure would be enough for Zack to be gone. Then, snapping branches under my toes, I made my way back to the road. Ciaran's car was there, but the keys were gone—they must have been in Ciaran's pocket. With no idea how to hotwire it, I set off on foot, headed in the direction I assumed was home. Of all the nights to forget my cell phone.

I don't know how long or how far I walked, but I finally found civilization. It was an old roadside tavern, which after the Prohibitions had been converted into a more Great Spirit–friendly meeting place. Young people sipped nonalcoholic cocktails and danced to a DJ playing Top 40 hits. I slipped in—no ID needed, though I did get odd looks from a few patrons. I found a college-age girl alone at the bar. "Can I borrow your phone?" I asked her. "I'll bring it right back." The kind of statement you had to tack on to prove your honesty to strangers—your unchanging face would prove you weren't lying. Sure enough, she handed it right over.

An outlet now in my hands, I thought of what to do. I should call the police, right? I stepped outside for privacy, nervous about what to say, how to phrase this kind of situation. I pressed the numbers 9-1-1.

"Nine-one-one, what's your emergency?" said a workman-like female voice.

My voice cracked as I said, "I think my friend got shot."

"What's your name and location?"

"I'm Grace, and he's not here anymore."

"He got up and walked away?"

"No, the murderer carried him away."

The operator was startled. "Murderer?"

"This guy came out of the woods and shot him."

The operator didn't know what to make of this. "He murdered your friend. And then was Punished so little, he was still able to carry your friend away?"

I was quickly realizing the futility of all of this. I was afraid to mention the pills, or Zack's name. I didn't know what Zack was involved in, so I didn't want anything to be easily traced back to me. But I tried one more thing. "He was Punished, but then he got better."

"He just got Forgiven on the spot?"

"I guess."

"So where is your friend now?"

I couldn't send them to Zack's house. Besides, I doubted he'd be keeping Ciaran's body in the closet, across the hall from his little sister. Though if he hadn't buried Ciaran here in the woods, I couldn't imagine what else his plan might be. So all I said was, "I don't know."

"If this is a crank call, you should hang up before your Punishment gets worse."

The operator's disbelief was enough to scare me into saying, "Never mind, I'm sorry."

I hung up, not sure what to do now. It was the middle of the night. The GPS on this stranger's phone said I was still miles from home. I was scared enough to make one more call—to my father, who I knew was still in D.C., an hour away.

Thankfully, he answered, a little dazed, barely awake. "Hey, Dad, can you come pick me up?" As I hung up, I began to panic. Somehow I was going to have to explain all of this to a cleric.

My dad arrived as the tavern closed, anxious out of his mind. "What happened to Ciaran?" he asked.

I was honest. "I don't know."

"He just left you at this bar? Alone?"

I would have told him everything, but my conversation with the 911 operator had made me wary. What I'd seen wasn't easily explainable, and my father was the last person I wanted judging me the way that operator had. So I stalled. "It's a long story."

"I'd like to hear it." There was that fathering instinct.

"It's okay, Dad. We had a fight. I'm just glad to be away from him now."

My dad sensed I didn't want to talk anymore. He let an uncomfortable silence settle in for a few miles, while I pondered what to do next. I remembered my father's explanations when Jude died, his desperate attempts to make sense of a world outside of what he understood, and how he'd failed me in that crucial moment. But still he was my best spiritual resource, so

I finally worked up the courage to ask him, "How does Great Spirit decide what's good and evil?"

My dad was quick on the draw. "The prophets of each country interpret Great Spirit's message . . ."

"But Great Spirit Himself . . . what if someone did bad things, but Great Spirit didn't Punish them?"

My father was confused. "Great Spirit Punishes all sinners."

I tried a different tack. "Let's say there was a way to avoid Great Spirit's Punishment. Do you know anyone who's done that?"

At this, my dad seemed to get concerned. "I know that the devil is still very much with us."

This was news to me. My father rarely spoke of the devil. The Universal Theology was much more positive, and talking of any higher power other than Great Spirit was frowned upon—the various deities of Hinduism, for example, were all said to be different manifestations of Great Spirit—there could be nothing else as powerful. So to hear my father talk like this now . . . I asked, "How? How is the devil with us?"

"He's vying for power in unseen ways."

I pressed him further. "Does the devil work like Great Spirit works? Can he make people beautiful and ugly? Why don't you talk about the devil, if he's still out there?"

Perhaps I'd reached the limit of my father's knowledge. Maybe he was keeping something from me, the way he often did. But he evaded my questions. Instead, he asked, "Have you seen something, sweetheart?"

I wanted to tell him everything. About Ciaran being blessed by Great Spirit, about Zack and the pills, all of it. And I was about to. It was on the tip of my tongue. But then my father continued, "You know the story of Job?"

"Of course."

"Sometimes we don't know why Great Spirit does the things He does. Sometimes He's simply testing us, to see if we'll keep the faith."

"Sometimes Great Spirit does terrible things, just to prove He can?"

"That's a very human way of looking at it. I don't think Great Spirit uses quite the same logic that we do."

I was no Job. I wasn't going to be able to keep the faith. The 911 operator, who would have heard if anything like this had ever happened before . . . even she thought I was crazy. How could I explain it to Paul Luther, the last person who would believe anything that might fly in the face of Great Spirit's word? And that's what everything I'd just witnessed was—the surest proof that everything I'd ever believed in was a lie. As I listened to my own thoughts, I began to feel a deep and immense guilt, the first time in my life I'd ever felt it—a guilt that perhaps I no longer believed in Great Spirit at all.

As I was thinking through this, my father looked at me, concerned. Casually, he added, "If you need to talk, let me know. You know how Great Spirit feels about those who doubt."

I glanced at my face in the side mirror and was shocked. I was deteriorating, slowly but surely. Being Punished. For my sins, for my doubt, for my dishonesty. And it was happening fast.

"We all lose faith sometimes," my father said. "Talking about it can help."

"I'll be fine." I craned my neck as far out of view of my father as I could. In the mirror, I watched my skin losing its glow, looking older, worn out. This Punishment was already far harsher than any childhood indiscretions, and because it was due to my dwindling faith, I wasn't going to be able to pray my way out of it, like I'd done so many times before. My father was right—Great Spirit Punished no one more harshly than those who doubted Him. This Punishment could kill me, and there was nothing I could do about it. I was in great, immediate, life-threatening danger.

As we got out of the car, and I began to drag myself to my now mercifully close bed, my father commented, perhaps trying to lighten the mood, "I like your coat. Is it new?"

"Yeah. Thanks."

I could only think of one way out of this situation. And I really, really didn't want to do it. I needed to get my hands on Zack's pills.

# CHAPTER 3

It was suicidal. Walking up to a murderer and saying, hey I saw you kill my friend, can I have one of your magic pills? Or to steal them . . . that could be even riskier. But I already had plans to carpool to school with Macy that morning, and when I woke up to see my face growing more and more ragged, my unbearably stupid plan began to form.

I drove over to Macy's in a hat and sunglasses, which ultimately did nothing but draw attention. When she opened the door, she could tell right away. She grabbed the sunglasses off my face and stared at me in shock. "What happened to you?"

"I lied to my dad," I said honestly. No need to make this Punishment worse for no reason.

"About what?"

"About where I went with Ciaran last night."

Before Macy could ask me anything else, another voice jumped in from the next room. "How'd it go?"

My heart skipped a beat as Zack entered the foyer. Watching

me, casually, as though nothing had happened, as though the boy he was asking me about wasn't the one he'd killed in cold blood last night.

I tried to keep my voice level. "You were right. I don't think we're soulmates."

Zack just stared. Trying to read me, maybe. "Sorry to hear that. It sounded like you liked him." He seemed so sincere. My spine tingled.

"I did."

Macy was busy rolling her eyes. "Weren't you leaving?"

Zack smirked. "Be nice to your big brother."

"I'd be nicer if you left."

"Why do you care?"

"Because Grace doesn't want to tell you about her date, she wants to tell me."

"I want to hear about Grace's date, too," he teased, looking at me expectantly. Was he really doing this to me? Did he know I knew, was he twisting the knife? Or was he fishing for information?

"What do you want to know?" I asked, as innocently as I could.

"What was he wearing? What were you wearing?" he asked jokingly, faux-girly.

Macy pushed him toward the door. "Uh-oh, you're late for work."

"Was he a good kisser?" Zack kept teasing.

Macy glared at Zack and stepped in front of me protectively. "Zack, go. Now."

Zack leaned around his sister and winked at me. "Fine, but I want the full report tonight." And then he left, to go to . . . work. To kill some other innocent kid? I didn't know what Zack's actual job was, and I was too scared to raise any red flags by asking Macy about it now. My father's words about the devil rang in my ears—could Zack be on the side of the devil? Killing off those Great Spirit had chosen for important roles in life?

I was torn from my tortured reverie by Macy. "Don't worry. Before we go to school, I'll fix your face."

The way she said it, I wondered . . . could Macy have these pills, too? Could they be some kind of family thing? I was full of hope. "How?"

"My secret formula." I followed her up to her room, where she pulled out . . . a makeup kit. No magic, just mascara. She continued, "I never thought I'd be doing this to you."

"Why not?"

She gave me a look like, *really?* "You're Grace Luther. Come on." I stared at my reflection. "Do you have to do this a lot?"

"Sure."

"For what?"

"Swearing. Sometimes I say mean things to my brother and Great Spirit gets mad. That's usually worth it though."

"That's it?"

She hesitated. And then she told me about a time when we were in middle school, when she'd volunteered to feed her neighbors' cat while they were abroad. Right before they returned to the country, Macy realized she hadn't been to see the cat in weeks. Though she quickly hurried over to feed it, not long after the owners returned, the cat died. Macy never told them she'd shirked her duties, and they never assumed she bore any responsibility. I tried to assuage Macy's guilt, but I knew I couldn't hide the shock and judgment on my face—not with makeup, not even with this Punishment. I wondered how many other things people had been keeping from me, thinking I was this Goody Two-shoes who couldn't handle it.

"Sometimes," she said, "when I think about it, that's when Great Spirit Punishes me. Just to remind me, I guess. But I've gotten pretty good at not thinking about it." She applied a final coat of lip gloss. "What do you think?"

My face did look better. "You're an expert," I said. I meant it as a compliment; hopefully she took it as one.

"Let's go. Makeup won't do us much good if we're both late for school."

As she headed for the stairs, we passed Zack's room. My opportunity was right in front of me, my best chance for survival. Makeup could only cushion the blow. If my body's deterioration continued at this rate, I'd be dead by nightfall. "Can I use your bathroom before we go?" I asked.

Macy nodded, and I headed back up the stairs, down the hallway. I closed the bathroom door to seem to anyone who passed like I was inside. Then I slowly turned the knob of the closed door next to it. Zack's room.

It looked like any young man's bedroom in any suburban home. The walls were still covered with posters of the bands Zack liked in high school. His debate club trophies. I'd never been in here before. It was cleaner than I expected. Perhaps that came with the occupation of trained killer.

I glanced under the bed and hesitantly opened a closet. No dead bodies, at least so far. No pill bottles lying on his dresser either. I took a cursory look through his drawers, didn't see any pills there, nor in the chest by his bed.

On the floor was a suitcase—his things from D.C., I imagined. I unzipped it. Rooted through his clothes. As much as Zack now terrified me, I still felt a twinge of guilt violating his personal property like this. After a few minutes of searching, I started to panic. Of course Zack's pills were well hidden. What if I never found them?

But before I could explore further, I heard a sound at the door, and I saw the doorknob turn. It was Zack.

# CHAPTER 4

I barely had time to jump under the bed as Zack entered and closed the door behind him. I was sure he must have seen me, must have been able to hear me. To my ears, my breathing was the loudest sound I'd ever heard.

But Zack continued his phone call—he'd walked in on his cell, and he put it on speaker as he searched through his drawers for something.

"Just give me one second—I can send the report now. Did you ever find a signal on the girl?" The girl. Could he mean me?

The voice through the speaker said, "We triangulated her cell signal to her house. She wasn't anywhere near the truck." Ciaran's truck. My cell phone was at my house when Zack murdered Ciaran. I *was* the girl. Could this mean Zack didn't know what I'd seen?

"Good. I just saw her. There's something going on for sure."

"You think she knows something?"

"Something, yeah. What, I don't know."

"Find out. Who knows what happened on that date before you got there."

"I just wish we knew what he was looking for in the woods, if it wasn't her." Zack paused. "Okay, it's sent."

"I'll forward it to the team for approval."

"Thanks, man. See you soon."

Zack turned off the phone and paused for a moment, maybe checking his email? My heart raced. *Please let him leave.*

Zack moved to his suitcase . . . would he notice that I'd moved the things inside, in my search? While crouching down to look at it, would he spot me hiding beneath the bed? I tried to breathe as quietly as possible—harder and harder with my constricting throat. Hiding here, trying to steal this clearly criminal medicine, must have caught Great Spirit's attention in a big way.

But as he unzipped the deepest compartment, he pulled out an electric razor—a perfectly normal-looking one I'd seen and tossed aside in my search—and removed the bottom. Out poured a handful of pills. What I'd seen in the woods wasn't a pill bottle at all; it was this contraption. He took one pill, then put the rest back in the razor. Which went back in the suitcase. I'd found them. As quickly as he'd entered, Zack zipped up the suitcase and left the room.

I got up, unzipped the suitcase, and opened up the razor, pouring some of the small, yellow, unmarked pills into my hand. The razor was full of them, hundreds at least. How many people was he killing that he needed all these pills?

His phone call had confirmed it: Zack was a part of some organization. But an organization that killed teenagers? It seemed impossible. Then a thought occurred to me . . . maybe Ciaran had been taking the pills, too—that would explain a lot. Maybe Zack and Ciaran were in rival gangs? Or . . . something? There were too many possibilities. Zack had the ability to track my cell phone signal, which scared me. And if they were tracking me . . . I had to get out of there.

I shoved the handful of pills in my pocket and quickly zipped up Zack's suitcase. I peeked out into the hall—empty, thank Great Spirit.

As I reopened the bathroom door, I checked myself in the mirror—I was starting to look disgusting. I wanted to take the pill then, but that would be too obvious, the sudden change. I had to make it through the day.

I walked slowly, evenly, trying to keep the pills in my pocket from rattling.

I could hear Zack talking to Macy as I entered the living room. "Where did Grace go?"

"Bathroom," Macy answered. "Why are you so obsessed with Grace?"

I paused, hoping Zack would answer before they noticed me, but he saw me first. "Macy thinks I'm obsessed with you."

Macy slapped Zack on the arm. "Don't tease her. She's had a bad day."

"I didn't say it, you said it."

"It's okay," I cut in. It came out wheezy, labored. For a moment I was sure that Zack could see right through me, that he knew I'd stolen the pills.

But then with an "Okay, you kids have fun," he was off. No concern for me anymore. Maybe whomever he'd talked to on that phone call had assuaged his worries. His interest in me was no longer pressing enough to stay and torture me. That was a relief. He'd pump Macy for information later, I was sure.

As we started the drive to school, Macy was ready for story time. "You slept with him, didn't you?" I shook my head. She was annoyed. "I told you my story. You have to tell me yours."

I did the best I could. "He tried to . . . you know. I stopped him. We got in a fight, and he left. I don't know where he went. Later when my dad asked me what happened, I was too embarrassed to tell him, and that's when I lied." That sounded like good information for her to pass on to Zack, and every word was true enough that I'd pass Macy's visual lie detector.

Macy was stunned. "What happened to Ciaran?"

"I don't know. I haven't heard from him today."

She asked carefully, "Do you want to?"

Did I want to hear from a ghost? "Definitely not. I was lucky things ended the way they did."

In the side-view mirror, out of the corner of my eye, I could see my face getting worse and worse. I could tell Macy wanted to ask me about the Punishment, but she was being considerate, worried about my safety . . . if thinking about her troubles affected her, she wouldn't want to prod me to do the same.

"Maybe you should skip school today. I'll cover for you."

"You can't do that." I wasn't letting anyone else get Punished for lying. This was my mess, and I had to take care of it.

"It's worth it. Whatever it costs me, it's worth it. If you go to a worship center, I know you, you'll pray this thing away in like an hour."

I hesitated, trying to find some way to keep her safe. "I'm sure I can find a junior cleric to write me a note."

"Perfect," she said. And then she gave me a hug. "It's gonna be okay."

Even though she didn't know the truth, she didn't know how bad it was, I teared up. "You think so?"

"You're Grace Luther. I know so."

"What do you mean, I'm Grace Luther?"

"You're the strongest one of all of us." She meant my group of friends at school, the pious ones who sat at the big lunch table right in the middle of the cafeteria. I wondered how many of them, at one point in time, had gotten her secret makeup treatment. For the first time since my terrible date, I didn't feel so alone.

"Thank you."

She dropped me off outside the nearest worship center— not my father's, of course. My instinct was to step inside . . . but then I remembered, I had a better solution. I waited for Macy to drive out of sight, and then I walked home. Slipped into my room and pulled out the pills. I was afraid. At that moment, I imagined how this might have gone if my mother was still alive. I could have trusted her, I thought. She would have understood, she would have given me advice and held my hand and made everything better. But the mirror reflected only one person—me. I wondered what side effects the pills might have. But I'd gone to all the trouble to steal them—I didn't have time for doubts.

I braced myself and slipped a pill into my mouth. For a moment, nothing happened.

Then suddenly, viscerally, I felt my whole body transform. My face became perfectly symmetrical, and my brown skin grew more radiant than I'd ever seen it, shining like a polished copper penny. I felt healthier and stronger than ever in my life. I felt relaxed, I felt powerful. I hadn't felt this good since I was nine years old, at the Moment of the Revelation, the very first time I was Forgiven.

With a whole pocketful to burn, I tried an experiment. I wanted to know if these pills protected me against future sins as well as previous ones. I tried the simplest sin I could think of and whispered, "Hell!" I waited. Usually, for me, this word was accompanied by an immediate response from Great Spirit—but not this time. I tried again. "Crap." Still nothing. I tried more vile expletives, anything I could ever think of having heard somewhere. It seemed I was now, like Ciaran, under Great Spirit's protection, no matter what I did.

In that moment, with the fear of death gone, the weight of everything I'd seen and experienced suddenly crashed down on me. The loneliness, having these secrets I couldn't confide in anyone—not my father, not my best friend. The confusion of a world I no longer understood. The only thing I had to hold on to, in that moment, was the knowledge that I'd somehow gamed the system, that I'd somehow found a way to beat Great Spirit.

All the guilt I'd ever felt melted away. I was angry. Angry about my mother's death, and Jude's. Angry that even though I lived in this newly just world, life still felt so unfair. But I had this new power, an unbridled ability—like Ciaran, like Zack—to take whatever I wanted, everything this life had always denied me.

And I was going to take advantage of that.

# CHAPTER 5

I didn't start right away. I waited to hear from Macy that Zack had stopped asking questions, but after she passed on my story about lying to my dad, it seemed that Zack lost interest completely.

My revived appearance seemed to soothe my father's concerns. I told him I'd been praying all day—a statement he didn't doubt, and a lie the pills kept me from revealing.

It seemed the pills had a time limit. My beauty would start to fade after a day or so, and I'd have to take a new one. I hadn't figured out exactly what to do when my supply ran out. But I was getting antsy . . . I knew I had a small window to take advantage of my newly opened world, perhaps the only one I'd ever have, and I wasn't willing to miss out on that.

The story of my disfigurement hadn't spread to anyone at school—Macy was inherently trustworthy. It was a good thing, obviously, to have my reputation intact. But at the same time, trying to act normal, when no one knows what you've experienced . . . it can get lonely. I think if I'd had Macy to talk to, who at least had seen the effects of my ordeal, I might not have needed to do what I did next. But by the time I was back in class later that week, she was out with the flu, and the isolation started to make me crazy. So that Saturday, I decided to take advantage of my newfound abilities.

It started with stealing my dad's car. I could have asked him to borrow it, and with my fancy new face he would have said yes to anything. But I enjoyed the rush of doing something unheard of, something no one had been able to do for a decade. I drove to the store, but there wasn't much to do there. It was hard to fly in the face of Prohibitions at 7-Eleven, where the raciest thing you could buy was *Vogue* magazine.

So I headed somewhere I knew I'd need these pills, somewhere I knew I'd see no one familiar, somewhere I had to navigate to based solely on my fuzzy memories. The black market.

Despite the immunity the drug conferred on me, I was wary of getting caught. As I drove to the Outcast side of town, I kept an eye on the cars around me. Cutting through side streets, I noticed someone following me—a motorcyclist with a blue full-face helmet. My heart raced as I took turn after turn, and the motorcycle remained on my tail. It must be Zack. He'd caught up with my lies and was coming to finish me off. But as I paused on the side of the road, the motorcyclist whizzed by me. A false alarm.

I recognized the site immediately when I finally found it. It looked less menacing in daylight, but I'd know that street corner anywhere. I walked toward those big dilapidated doors, the most beautiful person for miles. With those pills rattling in my pocket, I felt a sense of superiority. I could dabble in these Outcast vices and return to the real world, with no one the wiser. This must have been how Ciaran felt. Omnipotent. I could see why someone might want to stop people like him—people like me, now.

This time, I browsed the aisles with more purpose. I paused to examine the liquor bottles, as though I knew enough to tell them apart. My experience with alcoholics like Clint made me wary of purchasing any, even with my newfound invulnerability. Who knew what might happen if I got addicted and couldn't find more of these pills?

And then, like I'd conjured him just by thinking about him—there he was. Clint. Ciaran's dad. On the other side of this liquor shop, examining bottles with the eye of someone who *could* tell the difference. I paused to consider the astronomical odds, then realized: no wonder Ciaran had known about this place—his father would have been the one to take him here to begin with. It seemed Clint had abandoned his reformed self already. My lady volunteer friends would be so disappointed. His face showed he hadn't been back on the bottle long, but I knew it was only a matter of time before the drink would kill him, before Great Spirit would Punish him to death.

I quickly stepped away, but it was too late. He glanced my way, and I'm sure he saw me. I slipped between the aisles of raunchy movies, hoping to disappear. As I wound through the decades-old thrillers and pornos, I wondered . . . did Clint know what had happened to his son? Surely Ciaran's parents must have realized he was missing . . . did they know I was the last person he saw? If so, why hadn't they tracked me down? It had been almost a week now. Had they called the police, and if so, might my 911 call be unearthed?

I felt a responsibility to tell them, to give them some kind of explanation. But I knew it was too risky. Risky like being here. I was suddenly reminded of the stupidity of my behavior. I had barely escaped notice by Zack, and here I was somewhere so suspicious, it was like advertising my crime.

I leaned against a rack of comedies, the boxes covered with pictures of scantily clad women. My desire to buy something was gone. I just wanted to go home. I peeked out—the coast was clear. Clint hadn't come looking for me. I put my head down and worked my way through the crowd, toward the exit.

As I opened the doors, I saw a sight more horrifying than all these Outcasts put together—my own father sitting on the steps. Waiting for me. Too afraid to cross that threshold into sin himself.

"Hey, Dad."

He was livid. Terrified. "What are you doing here?"

My voice shook no matter how much I tried to force it to be casual. "Just walking around. A friend told me about this place, I thought it would be cool to see it. I didn't buy anything." I displayed my hands to show they were empty. "How did you know I was here?"

"My car's GPS." Of course it had a GPS locator.

"Why did you come looking for me? I'm fine."

"No. You're not."

I guess that was true. He held out his hand, and I gave him the keys. "I want to know what's going on."

# CHAPTER 6

I had never gotten a lecture before. Turns out I don't like them. For the whole car ride home and a good ten minutes parked in the garage, my father went on about how lucky I was that Great Spirit had spared me, and how worried he'd been, and the suspicious look he'd gotten from his Uber driver when he asked to be driven to the black market.

If I'd been smart, I would have apologized, but I was too angry. All my frustrations came barreling out at my father. "If Great Spirit doesn't care, why do you?"

My father was shocked. "Are you talking back to me?"

I looked up at the ceiling. "Hey, Great Spirit, do you care if I have opinions?"

"Grace!"

"See, He doesn't."

"This isn't the daughter who's lived in my house for seventeen years."

"People change," was all I could think to say. I desperately wanted to escape to my room, but my father was staring at me with accusing eyes.

"Has the devil gotten to you?"

"Dad . . ."

"I can't think of any other explanation for what I'm seeing."

"You want the explanation?"

As soon as I said it, I regretted it. Because I knew the only thing he could say would be "Yes, I do."

Deep down I hoped maybe he could help, maybe he'd know what to do when the pills ran out, maybe if he had all the details he could make sense of everything I'd seen. So I began, "You know that date I went on last week?"

My father immediately misunderstood. "Oh no . . ."

"No, not that." My father seemed reassured that my virginity was intact, at least. I braced myself to say the words that were so much worse than that. "He tried to force himself on me."

"Did Great Spirit protect you?"

"No! I protected me. I ran away."

"Good. I'm glad you're okay." In that moment, I was reminded that he was my dad after all. I felt safe; I was sure that I could tell him anything. "Is your date alive?"

My heart stopped for a moment. How could my father be so far ahead of my story? Did he know something he wasn't telling me? "What do you mean?"

"His Punishment. How bad was it?"

Oh. Of course. "He wasn't Punished," I said.

"That you saw."

"No matter what he did, nothing happened to him. He said

it was because he was blessed. That he could do anything he wanted, and Great Spirit couldn't touch him."

My father was unmoved. "He was lying, of course."

"But his face didn't change. If he was lying, why didn't his face change?"

"Great Spirit works in mysterious—"

"No, He doesn't!" I couldn't stand hearing that stupid phrase again. "Whatever Great Spirit's doing is just random."

"Grace . . ." my father warned.

"It's been happening to me, too." As soon as it slipped out, I regretted it—I saw the change on my father's face, his horror.

"Since when?"

"Since my date with Ciaran."

"How? Why is this happening?"

I imagined my dad pulling up to Macy's house, asking her parents a lot of questions, and then getting cornered by one of Zack's associates, the ones he'd talked to on the phone. No, telling my dad about the pills, and where I got them, was not an option. "I don't know how. But I do bad things, things I would have been Punished for a week ago, and I'm still beautiful. Just like Ciaran. He tried to rape me, he stole things, he drove without a seat belt—nothing happened to him."

"Maybe you just got confused after a bad date . . ."

"I'm not confused! I know what I saw."

"Great Spirit Punishes liars," he warned me gently.

"I'm not lying!"

My father was pacing the room. Not sure whether to believe my pious face. "I know it sounds crazy," I said. "That's why I didn't tell you before. I didn't think you'd believe me. Or you'd think I was mistaken, or that I'd done something wrong. But I know what I saw."

I'm not sure if my father heard any of this, because the next thing he said was, "Maybe we should find someone else for you to talk to."

"Who else would I talk to?" I asked.

"There are doctors for times like this, when people have experiences that don't make sense."

"I'm not crazy, Dad!"

"I'm not saying that. But sometimes, we can't help what we see. The brain is a very complex machine, and sometimes when one part gets out of place . . ."

"Fuck you!" I shouted. It was the first time I'd ever said that word, and my whole body tingled with excitement. I smiled, feeling powerful. "Look at my face. Is it changing? It's not changing."

My father looked at me with horror, took a step back.

"I'm sorry," I said, starting to feel guilty.

But my father's frustration and confusion had turned to rage. With a voice steady and intimidating, he said, "This is a house of Great Spirit, and you will listen to what your father says. Go to your room, and pray for Forgiveness."

"I don't need to be Forgiven, see?"

"Something has overtaken you. You've caught some kind of spiritual disease. Go to your room right now."

I gave up. Trudged upstairs. My father was going to be no help, and now he was watching my every move. I stared at the pills in my hand. They felt like a liability now. I'd had my fun, I'd gone to the black market, and it wasn't worth it. It wasn't worth ruining my relationship with my father, or the guilt I was feeling about defying Great Spirit. And if my father found the pills, figured out what they were . . .

I looked at myself in the bathroom mirror. It had been a day since my last pill, and my skin's healthy glow was already dimming. I could take another one, putting off the inevitable—or I could try to make amends to Great Spirit. Do some act of atonement. I stood in front of the toilet and dumped the pills in. For a moment I just stared at them, sitting in there, and considered swiping them out, putting them back. But then I gathered my courage and flushed.

They swirled away, down the drain. I glanced back to the mirror, expecting my reward—but nothing came. Great Spirit didn't care what I had just done.

I stayed in the bathroom looking at my appearance for almost an hour, waiting to see what would happen. But when the deterioration began, it progressed at lightning speed. Every terrible thing I'd done all week—I was being Punished for all of those things at once. Stealing Zack's pills, going to the black market. Great Spirit was angry at me for all of it. I realized then just how screwed I was.

The pills were gone. And without them, I was going to die.

# CHAPTER 7

I surrounded myself with every holy book I owned. Besides my standard Great Book, I had a Buddhist prayer wheel to one side, a statue of Ganesh on the other. I'd pulled out a set of Hanukkah candles—one of my last gifts from Jude, which I'd vowed never to burn. But in this dire moment, I thought perhaps they could help me. I liked the idea of his spirit being around me. That maybe, from beyond the grave, he could protect me somehow.

I wondered if this was what it had been like for Jude. He'd been lucky enough to be far from a mirror and miss the terrifying experience of watching his body disintegrate, but I knew he could feel it happening, just as I could. I remember that look in his eyes, knowing he was going to die, knowing it was the end. I didn't understand then why he wouldn't pray; now I did. When Great Spirit sends you the Ultimate Punishment, you know, deep inside. You know you're too far gone; you know you're beyond Forgiveness.

I didn't think I'd done anything so bad, logically. A little teenage rebellion. A couple trips to the black market. A few kisses with a boy who was not my true love. And a lot of doubt. But that doubt—I could feel it was fatal. I knew now why older people like my father were so paranoid, why every question I'd ever asked about Great Spirit was hurriedly answered with rote dogma—there was nothing more dangerous than doubt.

As I watched my face melt, my muscles wither, I knew it was the end. I prayed because I had to, because I wasn't capable of giving up, but I knew it would do no good. For the first time in my life, I could feel Great Spirit's indifference. I was saying empty words, and no one was listening.

As the last embers of the candles extinguished, and my strength diminished, I gave up on my father's plan. Maybe he was right, maybe those pills had come from the devil. But if the devil was the only one who could save me, I was ready to make a deal.

I snuck into the bathroom, futilely tried to stick my fingers down the throat of the toilet. The pills were long gone. I wondered where those pipes led to. Could I open the sewage line, wade through waste to find them? That thought didn't disgust me as much as it should have. The desperation of imminent death can drive you to unimaginable things.

A more logical plan emerged, one I'd already managed once before. I'd have to steal more pills from Zack. I fumbled for my cell phone. With the loss of muscle coordination, it was hard to maneuver. It was late, after midnight, and Macy didn't pick up. She must have already been asleep. I'd have to go there in person.

I grabbed my dad's keys—stealing the car again, another infraction Great Spirit would have to live with. But as I stepped into the driveway, I wasn't sure how I could possibly get to Macy's house. My legs were so weak they could barely support me, my arms useless as I struggled to open the car door. There was no way I'd be able to work the gas pedals for the six-mile drive. I couldn't get on the road without endangering every other car. Great Spirit would strike me down to prevent that, for sure.

I fell to my knees on the pavement. This would embarrass my father so much, I thought. Cleric's daughter, struck down by Great Spirit, right in the middle of our driveway. People would leave his worship center in droves. I'd be leaving him alone, I realized. My mother was gone. My father had devoted his life to his worship center, never come close to remarrying. Could he survive losing me?

I couldn't give up. I had to find a way to live, somehow. There was one person left to call. It was risky; it might be suicide in its own right. But it would be better than dying here as a useless lump in my driveway, too weak to move, throat closed up so I couldn't scream for help. I was going to have to call Zack.

It was hard work just to pull my phone out of my pocket. I had to put the phone on the ground, I was too weak to even hold it. I desperately fumbled at the screen. "Call Zack," I said to it with my garbled voice.

"Sorry. I didn't understand that."

"Zack Cannon," I squeaked out, as loud as I could through my constricting throat. Finally, the phone understood me. Dialed.

And then I noticed the battery life. I hadn't charged it since yesterday, I'd been so distracted.

"Hello?" Zack's voice asked me. But he couldn't ask me anything else—my phone was dead.

I lay down on the ground, on my back. I couldn't hold myself up anymore. I couldn't walk to find another phone. I was out of hope. This was it. I'd given up. I was ready to wait and see where I ended up in the next life—if this Punishment was enough, or if I'd spend the rest of eternity serving time for these few sins. I closed my eyes. A kind of dreadful peace.

My head spun as the lack of oxygen began to play with my brain. I felt myself being lifted up. I'd heard of near-death experiences, where people walked toward a light. This was different—it was physical, it felt like I was really moving. I wasn't sure in what direction—I felt as though I was being carried somewhere, but I wasn't sure if I was ascending, or simply preparing to descend. My heart fluttered. What happened next would decide my eternal destiny—a life spent in bliss or in flames.

But then I opened my eyes. This wasn't my soul traveling to the next world . . . this was someone moving my physical body. Someone was carrying me. A man—these were strong, masculine arms. They weren't my father's, that at least I could tell. But I couldn't see the face.

"It's okay, I've got you." I recognized that voice—deep and melodic. But it couldn't be. With my last ounce of strength, I strained my neck to see. It was an odd angle, a profile from below, and he looked very different from when I'd last seen him—he'd grown a beard, and his face had seen a lot of sun. But that jawline, that nose. I had to be hallucinating.

"Jude?"

And then I passed out.

# CHAPTER 8

I can't say for certain what happened next. I was in and out of consciousness, and what I do remember felt like a fever dream. One minute, I was in the passenger seat of my dad's car, speeding through town as I looked out the window, nauseous; the next I was a kid, sitting on my lawn with Jude, playing at being astronauts.

"Now we're going to Jupiter!" Kid Jude said.

"But we can't really go to Jupiter," I said. Even as a child, I was always very literal about my games. I only wanted to play pretend at things that could actually happen.

"Sure we can," Jude said. "We get in a rocket, and then we blast off."

"But where will we find the rocket?" I asked.

"We'll make one."

"I don't know how to make a rocket."

"You'll learn."

"How?"

"I'll show you."

And then I was back in the car, leaning against the window, and I could see the ground whizzing below us outside.

"Don't try to talk," the male voice in the driver's seat said. Was it Jude? Or was this a dream, too?

"Can you build a rocket?" I mumbled, trying to verify his identity, but I don't think he ever responded.

Suddenly I was a kid again, at our worship center, on the day of the American Revelation, and I could feel the heat around me. My father was up at the podium, preaching. "We're coming!" he shouted. "Leave the door open for us."

I turned to the mystery woman sitting next to me, the blonde who'd been with me at the Moment. My mother was in the bathroom; she'd be back any minute. "What does he mean?" I asked the mystery woman.

"We don't have much time," she said. "She's dying."

The next thing I remember, I was somewhere else. My eyes were closed. As I slowly came to, I realized I was on a couch with unfamiliar scratchy cushions. Where could I be? Everything felt so dreamlike. What if this *was* a dream? I began to hope . . . Could everything I'd just experienced be nothing more than a nightmare? Would I wake up and find Jude alive next door? Ciaran and the pills would never have existed, and Zack would still be Macy's harmless older brother, and everything would just be back to normal?

I lifted my head—it took immense effort—and opened my eyes.

The room was dark and quiet. Out of the corner of my eye I could see a woman. She was rummaging through her supply closet. "She's still breathing?" she asked. Something about her voice sounded so familiar . . .

My rescuer responded, "Just barely. The booster woke her up, but she needs something stronger." I couldn't tell where the voice was coming from. I tried to crane my neck to see, but I was too weak to support my own head. The woman approached with a small brown box.

But then she stopped. Squinted at my features. All Outcasts look the same. Or perhaps we didn't. She asked, "Who is that?"

"Why does it matter?" the voice asked.

"Just tell me."

"Her name's Grace Luther," the voice said, tentatively, as though he'd been found out. The woman backed away. "Why does it matter?"

"Luther?" The woman seemed panicked. "Paul Luther's daughter?"

"Yes," the man said, hesitant.

"Get her out of here. Get her out, get her out, get her out!" She threw the box down on the table and moved as far from me as she could.

"Dawn . . ."

"You brought her here? To my house?"

"I disabled the GPS on her dad's car . . ."

As they headed into the other room, I could hear their muffled conversation, drawers opening and closing. Finally, Dawn reappeared, walked over to me. The male voice began to panic. "What are you doing?"

I saw the gun in her hand, pointed at my head. Her voice steady. "I'm saving all of us."

# CHAPTER 9

The man stepped into view and pushed the gun barrel away. "Dawn!"

"It's the most humane thing to do. If I don't shoot her, she'll choke to death. It'll take hours. It's a miserable way to go."

"She's a good person. We can save her."

"Do you know who her father is?"

"He's a cleric, I know."

"One of the most important clerics in the country. Close to the prophet," she said.

"And because of that you're going to let her die?"

"People die every day through inaction. If we save her, more will die."

"Grace won't tell anyone," the voice insisted.

"She won't have to. Her father will recognize the signs, and he'll tell the prophet."

"You have to help her. You'll never forgive yourself if you don't."

Maybe it was that argument. Maybe it was another she made to herself. Maybe it was some conversation I wasn't conscious for, because I think I passed out again around this point.

But as everything blurred around me, I felt a sharp pain in my arm. I screamed. In my confused dream state, I saw myself locked in a torture chamber, imprisoned, stabbed with knives and spears and needles, as Dawn repeated, "This will be the end of us all."

I woke up in that same strange living room. There was air in my lungs. Strength in my muscles. An empty syringe next to me. I was alive. Against all odds, I was alive. There was a mirror on the wall by the door. My reflection was beautiful. Normal. Healed. And then I heard that familiar voice. "Are you okay?"

I turned. Next to me, in flesh and blood—it was Jude. Real, live Jude. I reached out, and my hand hovered an inch from his face. I was afraid if I touched him, he'd pop like a bubble, back out of existence. But he took my hand and touched it to his face. It was warm, scraggly and stubbly under my fingers. My mouth gaped open. "You're alive."

I stared, disbelieving. "How . . ."

But he didn't have time to answer before Dawn reentered the room. As she moved closer, I recognized that sharp, floral scent—she was one of the EMTs who'd responded to Jude's crash. The one who'd told me he was dead, the one who still comforted me in my dreams. Jude's resurrection was starting to piece itself together in my head.

"How are you feeling?" Dawn asked me. Her voice was soothing now, innocent . . . did she know I'd been conscious for her attempt to euthanize me?

"Fine, I guess."

"I'm sure you're confused right now."

No kidding. "What's going on?" I asked.

She looked me in the eye. "I'm going to be honest with you, Grace. You're in a dangerous situation. But I trust you, and I want you to trust me. Do you think you can do that?"

I hesitated. Could I trust her? I remembered everything my father had said about the devil. Could, despite her outward appearance, Dawn herself be aligned with the darkest of all forces? By letting her save me, had I made that deal with him? And more importantly, should I trust someone whose instinct was to shoot me in the head?

But then I looked over at Jude. He put a hand on my shoulder, reassuring. The touch was at once electric and terrifying—a ghost brought to life. And looking at my miraculously living, breathing friend, my curiosity was more powerful than my pious fear. I told her, "I can trust you."

"Good. Then I'm going to tell you the truth. The whole truth, as best as I know it. It's going to scare you, and it might put you in a great deal more danger. And what I tell you now you'll have to keep a secret from everyone. From your dad, from your friends, boyfriends, everyone. Are you okay with that?"

Maybe everything would have been better if I'd just said no. Maybe I could have escaped all the turmoil that was to come simply by leaving that room at that moment. But I didn't. "I want to know the truth," I said simply.

She took a seat across from me. "This world is not what you think it is."

# BOOK

## THREE

# CHAPTER 1

The prophet would like to meet with you." That was the phone call my father got in June of 2025.

This was before "the prophet" had a singular meaning in America, before Joshua's word was golden. At first my father assumed the caller meant Navid, the prophet of Pakistan, who'd taken on a more global role at the time by virtue of being first. But as the voice continued, my father realized he meant an American prophet.

With all the tumult happening around the world, you couldn't walk anywhere in the U.S. without tripping over a so-called prophet. Pakistan happened in late 2024, so by this time, the Revelations had spread throughout the Middle East and Asia, finally hitting the Caribbean in May of 2025. America's "prophets" were a dime a dozen, and they weren't just bums shouting on street corners—these were great evangelical leaders, saying the time of the rapture had come. Rabbis, imams, leaders of the New Age movement—they all had an opinion. They each believed they were the messiah meant to lead America out of the darkness.

But in every nation, it worked the same way—from the cacophony of voices, one would emerge with the backing of the prophets of the other nations. This man or woman, all the other prophets said, had a unique connection to Great Spirit and would take the lead in explaining Great Spirit's will to the people of that nation. And without fail, that prophet would predict the time and place of Great Spirit's Revelation in his or her home country. That's how in mid 2025, Prophet Joshua made his entry onto the world stage.

At the time, he was Joshua Villegas, a terribly unlikely candidate to lead the nation's religious future. He was an active member of a church in D.C., but he wasn't a minister. He had master's degrees in comparative religion and comparative government, and he'd spent most of his career working in a Washington think tank. Joshua had been quite successful—he had an ease with people, a charm with a five-mile radius. By the time he made his propheting debut, he had quite an impressive, if polarizing, record. He'd staved off wars and started one or two—always, he argued, on the side of the oppressed, looking for justice. And at thirty-nine, more than ten years younger than any prophet to come before him, he went from being one of the most powerful people in Washington to being one of the most powerful people in the world.

The media barely had time to speak the name Joshua Villegas before my father got the call, and instructions to show up at a construction site a few blocks from the White House—what would become Walden Manor, Prophet Joshua's famous residence. Joshua was working from a makeshift office in the back, away from the commotion. The prophet had one assistant keeping his schedule, Samuel Jenkins—you may have heard of him. By 2033, Samuel would have the honorific of "Guru," and as Joshua's right-hand man, he'd become one of the most powerful people in the country—almost a deputy prophet in his own right. This was the voice my father had spoken to on the phone. Samuel regarded my father with great deference and led him past all the heavy machinery to meet a handsome man, his nose buried in a thick volume. The man's dark eyes darted quickly over the page; he was so engrossed, he barely noticed as my father approached.

"Prophet Joshua? This is Paul Luther."

Even at the time, my father was impressed by Joshua. The man had a great spiritual presence, which would only grow with time and practice—he had an almost magical quality about him. Joshua had a thoughtful way of speaking, and a kind of social awareness that made it seem like he was reading your mind. Like his first words to my father, which were, "Apologies for the mess. We'll get real furniture next month, after the American Revelation."

My father was shocked at the casualness with which he said this. "Next month?" he asked. "It'll happen that soon?"

"Two fifteen P.M., East Coast time, on July 4," the prophet said. "Great Spirit figured we'd remember that one."

My father wanted to ask how he knew. My father prayed often, but God rarely gave him such specific instructions. Instead he said, "I'm honored you chose to contact me. But I can't figure out what you could want with a small-town pastor."

"You're a talented man," Joshua said. "And you understand what people want to hear." He said he'd visited churches, synagogues, mosques, ashrams. He'd scouted every religious leader in D.C. (and watched videos Samuel had recorded from thousands more all over the country), and he thought Paul Luther was the most talented speaker he'd seen. "In a week, there are going to be a lot of terrified people. You've seen how the Revelations have happened in other nations? The destruction, the loss of life, the terror and panic and mourning?" My father had. "It doesn't need to be like that."

"What do you mean?"

"Great Spirit is Forgiving. He doesn't want to Punish a single one of us. At the Moment of His Revelations, all of mankind is Forgiven, as long as they follow a specific set of instructions."

"That's not how it's looked."

"Because people have doubted. People have been afraid. To build this new world, only the faithful can remain. You understand?"

"Of course," my father said.

"I need your help to build that faith." Those were intoxicating words to a man who lived only to serve God.

"How?"

"We can save lives with the right message. I know your Christian faith already uses this word, 'saved.' But it means so much more now. I don't know if you know this, but I began my career studying the way people relate to God. And what struck me both now and then is how cocky we are. How we assume, with our tiny human brains, that we have any idea what He's thinking. How we look at this world of spiritual teachers and say, 'I know for certain which one of them is speaking the truth.' There's so little that the human mind can truly and fully comprehend in this world. But we have to find a story to make sense of things, we have to pick one truth or the other, otherwise we go mad. The truth is, I am but a vessel. As are you. As are we all. Great Spirit is trying so desperately to communicate with us, and we're ignoring Him. We ignore the teachers He sends because we are foolish. We are base. We are selfish. We could not follow even the most basic of His commandments, we could not stop ourselves from making war, we could not rein in our own greed and pettiness, and so now, we've brought this Judgment upon ourselves. This is our last chance. Mankind needs to listen, or we're going to vanish off the face of this earth. And mankind is only going to open their ears if the right people are speaking. You're that right person. And you and I need to find a lot more people like you, because otherwise, a lot of innocent people are going to die."

My father only had one question: "How can I help?"

The prophet had a message that he wanted everyone to hear, and my dad became devoted to spreading it. Paul Luther flew all over the country leading up to July 4, speaking to religious leaders on Joshua's behalf, helping them to prepare messages for their congregations. My whole childhood, I remember him speaking of the prophet like a friend, and I knew they worked closely together, but it wasn't until I was sitting across from Dawn that I realized just how powerful that made my father.

"I know you and your dad are close, and I'm sure you've never kept anything from him before"—*Almost true*, I thought—"but this time you'll have to. This time you have to make him believe that everything is exactly as it was before you met me. Because if a single word of this gets back to Prophet Joshua, we're all dead. Me, Jude, maybe even you."

"I understand," I said. More than anything, it was the way Dawn spoke about Prophet Joshua that worried me. Normally, people's voices are full of a kind of reverence when they speak his name, but hers wasn't. Hers was matter-of-fact, like she was speaking about any historical figure. He could have been William McKinley, he could have been Alexander the Great, he could have been Mussolini . . . no difference.

I could have run straight to my father the moment I was healed . . . yet here I was, talking to a mysteriously irreverent woman, and the more we spoke, the more I worried I'd accidentally aligned myself with the wrong side. But I was already in so deep, and everything she said was so different from everything I'd been told my whole life—her words were addictive. No matter how pious my heart wanted to remain, I couldn't force my body to leave. Especially not after she said, "Are you ready to learn the truth? About why people are Punished?"

# CHAPTER 2

What's happening to everyone, these physical transformations, this Punishment and Forgiveness . . . you've probably guessed by now. It's more complicated than it seems," Dawn said.

"How so?" I asked, nervous about what the answer might be.

"We've been doing research, and we can identify the process causing these changes . . . and it's scientific, not religious. This is something man-made, not Great Spirit."

She gave me a moment to process this. I'm sure I must have known, the moment I saw Zack take that pill—that was where all that doubt had come from. But I'd never put all the words together in a row like that. "It's not Great Spirit," I said, hearing how they sounded together. "Great Spirit isn't Punishing us. He never has been."

She must have seen the horror and revulsion on my face, because she quickly added, "Now that's not to say that Great Spirit doesn't exist. Most of the people I work with who know the truth still believe in some god or another. But this so-called evidence of His work, the *proof* that He exists—it's just not true."

"If it's not Great Spirit, what's causing it?"

"We're still working on isolating the exact cause, but we've found that changes in appearance directly correlate with feelings of guilt, and the chemicals associated with it that are released in our brains. That's what that drug we gave you did—it affected your brain chemistry."

My instinct was to reject her words outright. I'd been taught my whole life that faith could tell me more than science. Already my mind was spinning in somersaults, trying to find ways to prove her wrong. "How do you know? How can you prove that?"

"We've done tests. Hundreds of tests, hundreds of subjects, and they all come back the same. Aside from variations in individual biology, of course."

The pieces were falling into place, against my will. "So every time we do something bad, we feel guilty? And that's why the Punishment happens?"

Jude chimed in, "Even though the car accident wasn't my fault, I still felt so guilty for that kid's death, for hurting that woman . . ." He stopped, choking up a bit. "But it wasn't a judgment from the outside. It was my own judgment of myself." I moved closer to him, putting a comforting hand on his very real arm. I still couldn't believe he was sitting next to me.

"It's a shame," Dawn said. "Punishment is often a sign that someone's a good person, that they're capable of great empathy. They've recognized that they made a mistake and hurt someone, and that ends up being their downfall."

"So that's why Punishments don't affect everyone equally?"

"Exactly. Because everyone's brains are different. And everyone is raised with different cultural beliefs, which is why we need prophets. At least one in every country, to account for all those differences. Without prophets, people wouldn't know what to feel guilty for. Punishments wouldn't look like Great Spirit, they'd just look like random destruction."

"What about when Punishments are lifted? I've prayed myself better. How can that possibly be brain chemistry?"

"But that's just it. We've known for decades that prayer has a huge effect on the brain. You can put someone praying or meditating in an MRI machine and, over the course of weeks, you'll see the amygdala shrink, higher brain functions increase."

"So the way my brain changes when I pray . . . that's what makes me get better?"

"Exactly."

"What does that mean? Isn't that Great Spirit healing me?"

"In a way. You know, your brain doesn't know how to distinguish between an experience it imagines and one that's actually happening. If you imagine eating an apple—biting into it, chewing it, tasting it, swallowing it—your brain reacts as though it's a real apple you're eating. So an atheist might argue that the feelings associated with prayer are entirely created *by* the brain—that it's simply a mental state you cultivate, and that the apple, Great Spirit, is imaginary. But a religious person like you would say no, prayer is simply the brain's response to interacting with the divine. That whatever's going on in your brain is a response to something real, that you're actually eating the apple, so to speak. To be honest, it's not something we have the technology to distinguish yet."

Jude saw I was still confused, and tried to help. "Basically, science can't prove if there's a god. But scientists *have* figured out that the chemicals the brain releases when you pray can somehow counteract the ones that cause deterioration. That's what we just gave you—prayer chemicals."

I shook my head, still confused. "I still don't understand. How does feeling guilty make me ugly? What's actually causing the ugliness?"

"We don't know," she admitted. "Our research is still in progress."

"They're getting close," Jude said. "I met one of the scientists, Dr. . . ." He looked at Dawn, asking for approval to share the doctor's identity.

Dawn gave it. "Alexandra Smith."

"She's got all these experiments going . . . they're gonna figure it out."

Dawn could see my frustration, and she quickly added, "You're right that we're missing a piece of the puzzle. And until we find that piece, every solution we can concoct will be a stopgap. We're able to treat the symptoms—we can stuff people full of happy chemicals—but that's not a long-term plan. Until we know more, we won't be able to stop the Punishments of every person on Earth."

"Why don't you just tell everyone?" I asked. "Why let people go on believing something that kills them?"

"You think we haven't tried that? You know what happens when you tell people the truth? The first thing they do is question 'Great Spirit,' His power, His very existence. And you know what happens to those people?"

I did know. The same thing that had almost happened to me when I began to suspect the truth, when I was racked with doubt. "They die."

"They die, before their rational minds can catch up and process what we've told them. Fear and guilt take over. It's brilliant. It's the one conspiracy you can't go public with, because it kills anyone who learns the truth. To go on TV and proclaim to the world what's happening? If you were successful at getting your message out there, it'd be genocide."

"So what do you do?" I asked, feeling hopeless.

"We give people these," Dawn said, pulling a bottle of pills out of the brown box. They were different from the ones I'd found in Zack's suitcase. These were larger, cruder, red instead of yellow, but she promised, "They have the same chemicals that your brain naturally produces through prayer. They help people through that initial questioning stage, until they've adapted to a world where they don't have to constantly fear Great Spirit." They sounded the same as the pills I'd gotten from Zack.

Jude handed me the bottle. "You don't have to take them forever. I don't anymore. Once you're off them, you'll still feel guilty when you do something you regret, and your appearance will still change . . . but as long as you don't feel that doubt . . . that's what will kill you."

"Why?"

"We think it works like a feedback loop—the more you see yourself being Punished for your doubt, the more you feel guilty about doubting. That's our theory. But again, you don't have to believe in Great Spirit to survive without the pills—I haven't taken them in years. But it's been years since I worried that my agnosticism would send me to hell. I used to feel guilty, and I don't anymore."

"So the doubt, the guilt, will go away?" I asked.

"Eventually. I promise," she said. "Your only job right now is to convince your dad you know nothing."

And then I asked the question that worried me most. "Does my father know the truth?"

"No way," Jude said immediately. "If he saw how sick you were when I found you, he'd have found a way to help you. He never would have put you in danger. He loves you."

To my relief, Dawn nodded her agreement. "If he hasn't figured it out by now . . . I don't think he wants to."

"You think he's just in denial?"

"Your dad's a true believer," Dawn said. "Sometimes, it's easier to lie to ourselves. No one wants to believe they're wrong about everything they've believed in their whole life. When confronted with ideas that challenge their beliefs, most people will find ways to discredit those ideas."

I still didn't quite believe it. With the little I knew about science at the time, her explanation was as fantastic to me as any religion—more so, because religion was a language I'd been brought up to speak fluently. But brain chemistry . . . at the time it was just a bunch of big words I had to accept as fact.

This was the point where Dawn grew very serious. "You can't tell anyone what you learned tonight. You can't speak about any of this over the phone, or by email or text. Nothing that can be traced. We don't know yet who might be watching."

"I understand," I said.

"Good. Because in the next week, I promise you, you'll want to ask me questions, and I need you to understand that you can't. After tonight, you'll never see me again. So anything else you're worried about, please say it now."

I had a couple of questions, I'm sure . . . I don't remember now exactly what they were. Days, even hours later, I thought of a thousand things I wished I'd asked her. Why was Pakistan first? How did Joshua become prophet? How do you know everything you know? Why should I believe you? Who else can I trust? And most importantly—who can't I trust, under any circumstances? Not knowing the answers to those questions was going to put me in danger sooner rather than later.

"Normally," Dawn said, "I wouldn't send you home. You'd go into hiding, you'd give up your identity and assume a new one."

I looked at Jude—that must have been what he'd had to do to stay alive. "Why do I get to go home?" I asked.

"Because I think you could be the most valuable asset we've ever had. If you can help us, with your position close to the prophet—I think you could do some real good for people."

Though I had no idea what it meant, I liked the sound of it. Doing real good. But Dawn was right. Changing everything you believe in? It's not so easy, it never happens fast. No matter how much I nodded along with what she said, I was still trying to find a way to justify everything. Like a white blood cell encountering a virus, my emotional immune system was trying to protect me, to find a way to avoid having been so wrong. Not that I could have understood that or admitted it at the time.

Dawn saw all this running across my face and said, "You don't have to decide now." I nodded, relieved.

Jude took my hand. "Come on. I'll drive you home."

I nodded. Home. Where little did I know that at that very moment, my father, who loved me very much, was on the phone with Walden Manor, telling them everything.

# CHAPTER 3

My father had always had many questions about the devil. However, the prophets were universally mum on the subject, and they asked their clerics to keep the devil out of their sermons.

"We can all see what Great Spirit does. But the devil's work is usually invisible," Joshua would say. "To speak the devil's name is to imply the fallibility of Great Spirit. If anyone can challenge even a tiny bit of Great Spirit's domain, Great Spirit cannot be all-powerful. So that's why it's up to a few of us, the all-faithful, to fight that battle for Him, so the rest of humanity never has to doubt Great Spirit's power." My father understood this, even if he didn't like it. He had seen plenty of people succumb to the damaging effects of doubt.

So while I was upending everything I believed in, my father was on Skype, arguing with the prophet's right-hand man, Guru Samuel Jenkins. Unlike my father, Samuel was in no way humble about his connection to the prophet. And after all my father's years of service, he was annoyed to have to communicate with Joshua through this intermediary—he thought he deserved a direct line. "It's urgent. I need to speak to him right away," my father told Samuel.

"If I determine your case warrants an audience with the prophet, I'll arrange a meeting."

"It's my daughter. Something's . . . wrong."

"Oh?"

My father decided to come straight out with it. "She's been telling these stories . . . a boy who does terrible things but can never be Punished . . . have you heard of anything like this?"

"Who is this boy?"

"Ciaran something. Just a high school kid. I met him—there's no doubting he looks pious . . ."

"But you never saw him do anything bad?"

"Not myself, but my daughter . . ."

"Perhaps your daughter is exaggerating."

"That's not like her."

"Teenagers can be dramatic."

My father was nervous to relate what he'd seen—he didn't want to out me as a heretic—but he was more nervous that it would happen again. "It's happening to her, too."

This piqued Samuel's interest. "So you have seen it."

"Once. She didn't do anything terrible. Just swearing, nothing bad," my father said, trying to defend me.

"You should bring her here."

"To Walden Manor?"

"Yes. I want to see this for myself."

"Of course. And if you can't solve the problem, we'll set an audience with the prophet?"

Samuel smiled, placating. "Yes, of course."

# CHAPTER 4

As we left Dawn's house, I couldn't help but stare at Jude. It was surreal. How many times had I sat next to him, and here we were, doing it again—as though it were just another drive home from school. He was different now though—the ease of his gait, the seriousness with which he spoke. Even the way he dressed—casual, simple, like he wanted to recede into the background.

There was so much I wanted to know. "How did you survive?"

"Dawn and her friends. They saved me."

"How?"

He described that moment I remembered, after our car crash, when he was loaded into that ambulance, no hope left . . . and then something I wasn't witness to: a priest standing over him as the ambulance raced to the hospital. That little white collar was an unusual sight—most people had given up the physical trappings of their old religions. But this devout Catholic hadn't.

He was like many, I'd come to find out, who had never abandoned their old faiths—who worshipped, covertly, as they had pre-Revelation.

"My name is Father Dennehy," the priest told Jude. "And I have to ask you to make a choice." It was a conversation much like the one I'd had with Dawn—this one laced with a few more Our Fathers and Holy Spirits, but the message was the same. "Jesus will save you," Father Dennehy told him, "but you must repay the favor." Jude nodded, though he didn't then and never would believe that Jesus was anything more than a long-dead rabbi. The priest placed a red pill in Jude's mouth, and as the ambulance rolled away, Jude felt the drug work its way through his system. Saving him.

Jude looked up at Father Dennehy, amazed. "How . . . ?"

"You have been worshipping false idols. The world is not what you think it is," Father Dennehy said. Jude learned that Dawn ran a network of EMTs with a tap on the city's 911 calls. If they got word of a potentially fatal Punishment, they'd send someone like Father Dennehy to intercept the dying patient. Once the victim was safely in hiding, they'd show their families the body of a different dead Outcast, then bury an empty coffin, or deliver an urn filled with nonhuman ashes.

People like Dawn and Father Dennehy couldn't risk being caught—the prophet had methods for dealing with heretics like them—but they could still act under the radar and save lives.

So that was the bargain Jude made. He promised to go into hiding and spend the rest of his life helping others like himself, who'd suffered brutal consequences for their mistakes. Jude chose life . . . and gave up his old one.

"How have you been helping?" I asked.

Jude was vague—he pointed out what he'd done tonight, rescuing me from death. "Things like that. Riding in ambulances, passing out pills." But he wouldn't elaborate on any other people he'd saved—perhaps, I imagined, to protect their identities.

I realized, "My 911 call. That's why you were following me."

"I recognized your voice, yeah. Normally I stay out of town, to avoid being seen by anyone who might recognize me, but . . . once I realized you were in danger, I had to keep an eye on you."

I still had so many more questions. Where had he been for two years? Who was he, now that so much time had passed? Jude had always been so sweet, so kind, so endlessly forgiving of my faults and frustrations. But now he was walled off, and he shut down any additional queries I tried to make about our time apart. Sensing my concern, he said, "I'll tell you soon, I promise."

But I couldn't hold back my curiosity. "How big is this? How many people know?"

Jude hesitated. "I'm not sure what I'm allowed to tell you." And then after some prodding, "There are more. I don't know how many."

"In D.C.?"

"All over the world. All kinds of people. All these different religions that have survived, people still praying to Ganesh and Allah and Buddha. A lot of atheists who survived the initial Revelations."

"All working together?" Though I was living in a golden age of world peace, that peace was based on one thing—everyone living under one god, Great Spirit, one religion. I couldn't fathom people working together like that while believing in such different things.

"Yeah. They have churches, mosques, synagogues, ashrams, all in secret. All these people who have no identities in the real world, people whose families think they're dead, like me. That's why Dawn got so scared when I brought you in. Because she's worried if she goes down, all these other people who are saving lives will get caught, too."

"I won't get anyone caught. I promise."

I wasn't sure if Jude believed me. Perhaps he was doubting his choice to save me. I wondered what had changed since that drive two years earlier. If he still wanted to ask me the same thing he'd been about to ask then. I couldn't help but work in, "Before the car accident, we were talking."

"I remember," he said, as though he'd been waiting for me to bring it up.

"What were you going to say?"

He paused so long, I wondered if he'd heard me. He finally said, "I want to have this conversation. I really do. But you should know, after I drop you off, that's it. I'm not alive, you know, I'm living this whole other life, and to keep you safe you can't be a part of it."

"But I know everything now."

"It doesn't matter. I've spent the past two years wanting so badly to see my family and my friends, and I can't, because then people would know I survived, and they'd ask questions, and . . ."

"I won't give away your secret."

"You wouldn't have to. They'd track your phone, they'd . . ."

"I'll leave my phone at home. Please. I don't want to lose you again." I started to get angry. Not just at his stubbornness now, but at those years I'd grieved for him—pain I'd experienced for no reason at all. "You make this decision like you're the only one it affects, like there aren't other people who care about you who deserve a say. You can't just cut yourself out of people's lives . . ."

Jude took my hand. "Someday, this will all be over."

I looked at his face, instinctively checking to see if he was telling the truth. But none of his features changed, so maybe he believed what he was saying. Though what did I know about telling truth from lies anymore?

As we pulled up around the corner from my house, I hugged him tight. "Please just stay here with me. As long as you can." Having Jude back almost hurt more than losing him in the first place. I'd taken Jude for granted before the accident. I had forgotten how much I enjoyed his company, how safe he made me feel. Now that he was sitting next to me, all those old feelings came rushing back. How silly I felt for thinking Ciaran, or even Zack, could compare.

"I should go," Jude said. But he didn't, yet. He held my face in his hands. That moment, so close to him, I noticed a hundred things I never had before. How his brown eyes were a mile deep, with little flecks of a whole rainbow of colors. How long his eyelashes were. The way his fingers touched my cheek, so strong and so gentle. I wanted him to kiss me more than anything in the world. But he didn't.

And then I remembered—I was no longer constrained by any rules. There was no Punishment to be afraid of if Jude was not my soulmate. And what did I care now about the societal rules of boys kissing first? All I could think was that after all this grief and confusion, Jude was the one bright spot that had emerged from the darkness, and I wanted to hold on to him. I'd lost him once before . . . I knew I'd always regret it if I didn't take this chance. I leaned in, but before I could kiss him, he pulled away. Serious, businesslike. "I'll keep an eye on you. I won't be able to stop doing that."

I hid my disappointment as I sat back. "Thank you."

And he was out of the car, hopping on a motorcycle he'd left hidden in the nearby bushes. He pulled on a blue motorcycle helmet. A familiar one. It wasn't Zack who had been following me to the black market . . . it was Jude. Jude's ghost had been with me after all, who knows how many times. "You're not alone" were his final words to me.

But then he rode off, and he was wrong—I felt so alone.

# CHAPTER 5

As I pulled in my driveway, I could see my father moving around in the kitchen. Had he waited up all night for me? I steeled myself, prepared my story.

The drug rushing through my veins relaxed me. Dawn had explained it was like a very precise form of Xanax, a drug I'd never heard of until that night. For those of you born after the Revelations—Xanax was a drug used in the twentieth and early twenty-first centuries to treat anxiety disorders. Antidepressants were among the surprising early Prohibitions by Prophet Joshua—perhaps, I realized, for this very reason—that they would interfere with the chemicals in the brain that created Great Spirit's Punishments.

Though antidepressants took some time to work their way out of society, a drug that was mainstream when I was born was, by 2033, nearly nonexistent, except perhaps at black markets. And if those old anti-anxiety medicines were a hacksaw, this new one was a scalpel. Not only did these mysterious red and yellow pills prevent you from experiencing the physical changes associated with guilt, they blunted the guilt itself. No wonder I'd felt so comfortable going to the black market, I realized—the pills had chemically wiped my conscience clean. I could see why Jude was so insistent that eventually I stop taking the pills—what they might do to a person seemed dangerous. But in this moment, facing my father, they were going to be very helpful. I knew I needed to sell him on my holiness and naïveté, and I had never felt more prepared to say whatever was necessary.

As I walked in, I played cool to my father's shocked face. "Grace! Thank Great Spirit."

"You were right," I told him. "I'm so sorry. I prayed for a long time, and Great Spirit Forgave me. The thing that's been happening—it's not going to happen anymore. I'm sorry for taking the car without asking . . . I just thought, if I drove out to the place where I had that bad experience with Ciaran and prayed there, maybe I'd get some clarity. And I did." The lie came out smooth and clean. No hesitation, not a word out of place. Never had I lied with such ease, with so little remorse.

My father hugged me, relieved. "I'm glad you're okay."

"I understand why what I did was wrong, and I won't do it again."

As my father pulled away, I saw the conflict on his face. "I have a confession to make." I kept my breathing even and calm. I would have to appear surprised no matter what he said. "I was really worried about you, so I made a phone call."

"To who?"

"To some of my colleagues. I thought they might be able to help."

"I'm fine now," I insisted.

"I believe you. But they're concerned about you. They'd like to hear your story. I'm sure you have some questions. Maybe you can ask them. Get some closure. I'm sure you're tired of hearing the same old answers from me."

"Who am I asking?"

"That's the most amazing part. It's an audience at Walden Manor later today with Guru Jenkins."

"You're kidding." I hoped my terror came off as excitement.

"There are a few benefits to being a member of the spiritual community," my father said.

"I'm really tired," I said, needing to get out of there.

"Go take a nap. I'll wake you up when it's time to get ready."

"Thanks."

It was all I could do to get out of that room and into mine, door closed, mind spinning. After only an hour, I was desperate to contact Dawn again, just to ask her for advice. Were the prophet and his associates to be trusted? My gut said no—if Joshua was the leader of a religion based on a falsehood, something didn't feel right about that. But if they weren't to be trusted, why hadn't she mentioned that? Was Samuel as in the dark as my father was? What would he feel justified in doing if he thought I was allied with the devil? Or worse, if he was part of this whole conspiracy, what would he do if he knew I knew the truth?

If it really was the truth. I started to resent Dawn. Protect us at all costs, but we can't do a thing for you—that was basically what she'd said. Why should I trust her? I ran my fingers over the bottle of red pills she'd given me to take until I stopped needing them. Those pills, and my life, were Dawn's promises of loyalty.

I considered . . . if there was a devil, this is what it would look like, right? A friend rising from the dead. A mysterious coalition of blasphemers, shrouded in secrecy, who had to be convinced to let you live. Now that Jude was gone, he seemed so much less tangible. The whole experience still retained a dreamlike quality—could I have made up the entire thing? Why had I been so quick to believe this relative stranger and this seeming apparition over my own father, a man I implicitly trusted, whose word I'd believed as gospel my whole life? Why had I confided such dangerous secrets in them?

Either way, I was going to have to face Samuel Jenkins. I knew Jude was gone, off to wherever it was he lived now. But I hoped somehow he could see my one last cry for help, that his promise of watching out for me would come true now when I needed it to. I rummaged through my closet, found my old blue bear, and set it in the window with a newly recorded message: "I have a meeting today at Walden Manor." As it looked out at the murky dawn, a beacon to a lost friend, the last kind of prayer I knew how to make, I lay in bed, willing myself to sleep, hoping that when I woke, there would be some kind of answer waiting for me.

# CHAPTER 6

I slept fitfully, and after an hour or so, I couldn't force myself to sleep anymore. I looked outside—the teddy bear was unmoved, with no new response recorded. I was going to have to face Samuel without help.

I tried to remember what I'd told my father about Ciaran. I was sure he'd told Samuel every word. I rehearsed my story: I'd relate the bare minimum of facts about my date, and I'd leave out anything about Zack or Jude or Dawn. I'd play dumb. I'd play me two weeks ago.

I pulled on my most conservative dress, the one I wore to our worship center for Ramadan break fasts. I took a pill and hid a second in my shoe, just to be safe. Getting antsy, I headed downstairs, where my father was emailing his sermon to the junior cleric who was covering for him today.

"You're up. I said I'd wake you."

"I couldn't sleep."

"It's exciting, isn't it? The prophet's an amazing man. Just standing in his presence is enough to heal you." I'd seen the videos on TV. Blockades holding back hordes of Outcasts, all reaching to touch Joshua's hand. For the one or two who were lucky enough to make contact, their whole bodies would change, instantly. "Maybe if we're lucky, we'll get to see him today."

"That would be cool," I said.

As we sat in the car, en route to Walden Manor, I grew more antsy. The truths I'd learned from Dawn barely amounted to anything, when I thought about it. She hadn't told me much more than I could have guessed just by knowing about the existence of these stupid pills. And she'd shown no evidence to back up her claims. Couldn't it still be Great Spirit acting on all of us, I wondered, even if it was related to guilt? Wasn't everything Great Spirit, really? And if she couldn't tell me how she knew what she knew, why should I trust anything she'd said?

I'd made a promise not to betray her, but hadn't she betrayed me, in a way? Hadn't she abandoned me with all these questions? I knew Great Spirit was vengeful . . . would He Punish me for withholding information about potential subversives, people who were spreading lies about the Universal Theology? Maybe all of my problems would last until I did something that won Great Spirit's approval again. Maybe all I had to do was tell Samuel the whole truth, tell him everything about Zack, and Dawn's organization. But then I remembered the last time I'd tried to win Great Spirit's approval—and it had ended with me nearly dying in my driveway. No, I was going to have to lie, and hope I was good enough to get away with it.

As we walked up the D.C. block crowded with tourists, I averted my eyes from the Outcasts, mostly homeless, on the streets around Walden Manor. "On Fridays, that's when you see scenes like that blockade on TV," my father explained. "That's the only time the prophet grants miracles without an appointment."

There was a line of Outcasts outside the entrance, leading to a line of security guards with guns holstered at their hips. They looked battle-tested—who knew what desperate Outcasts might do to come close to Prophet Joshua's healing touch? We stepped to the front of the line, flashed our IDs, and a bald, tough guard with ice-blue eyes matched us to a list. The guard watched me carefully, and a shiver went down my spine. "Grace Luther?"

"Yes," I said.

As he ushered us inside, my father explained, "It's easier for us to get through because of how we look. They know we aren't lying."

*Do they?* I wanted so badly to ask. *Don't these guards know what I know? Shouldn't they be in on whatever this great lie is?* But I didn't. We walked through the beautiful hallways, lit by stained-glass windows and filled with religious artifacts from around the world.

But then we reached a second security checkpoint unlike anything I'd seen before. It reminded me of airport checkpoints in the pre-Revelation era—metal detectors and other mysterious machines. I wondered what those machines scanned for. Could they sense the chemicals coursing through my bloodstream? A long line of Outcasts waited to go through them, people who looked like I had yesterday, barely able to hold themselves up. I wondered if they would survive that line. I wondered if I would survive this trip. I felt a wave of nausea and dread. "Are you okay?" my father asked.

"I'm not feeling so good," I said honestly.

"There's a bathroom right around the corner."

"That's a good idea."

I slipped into the bathroom. The cooler air inside calmed my stomach a bit. There was only one other woman in there, a masculine-looking Outcast in a billowy purple dress, carefully applying lipstick. She gave me a sidelong look as I entered. It was funny, how vanity remained even when one's face was unrecognizable.

I slipped into a stall, caught my breath. I could do this. I stared at the deep green tile floor, practicing my story in my head. I knew what I had to do, what I had to say. I was ready. As I opened the stall door—WHAM. The door pushed back in on me. The Outcast woman was now in the stall with me.

"What do you want?" I asked her fearfully. Her brown eyes, strangely familiar, pierced mine. She put a finger to her lips and closed the stall door behind her.

Finally, she spoke. "Grace. It's me."

# CHAPTER 7

I didn't recognize her. But then she spoke again, and I recognized her deep voice. "I can't stay long."

This was no woman—it was often nearly impossible to distinguish the gender of Outcasts' faces. "Jude?"

He put a finger to his lips. I couldn't help myself, blurting out, "What happened? Why do you look like that?"

"I got your message. It was the only way to get in and see you."

"But why do you look like . . ." What sin had he committed, on my behalf, to deserve such Punishment?

"There are drugs that go the other direction, too," he explained.

"You've been waiting for me here?"

"Since I got your message." He'd found the bear.

I teared up. "Thank you."

"You're going to be fine. As far as we can tell, Samuel doesn't know anything besides what your father told him. Don't accept what he gives you to eat or drink. As long as you tell him what you told your dad, you'll be fine."

"Okay."

"Are you afraid?" he asked. I nodded. "That's okay. Most people are nervous to meet high-ranking clerics. You'll seem authentic."

"Should I be? You keep saying I'm in danger. Is Guru Jenkins a bad guy? Is the prophet?"

Jude shook his head. "Just be careful, and you'll be fine." He saw that I was still afraid and added, "I know it's been scary, but it's almost over."

He hugged me, and I wanted to hide inside his arms. I hadn't told him or Dawn any of what had happened with Ciaran . . . they didn't know what had caused my near deadly Punishment, and they'd never asked. I wanted to confide in Jude now about everything . . . but feeling his warmth up against me, I couldn't bear to tell him about a kiss with another boy. So I simply said, "Aren't you in danger, being here?"

"I'll be fine." I knew that didn't mean no. I was so grateful, so moved. It had been mere hours since I'd touched his handsome face, and now his cheek felt so cold under my fingers, the skin dry and damaged. But his eyes—those eyes were the same. And though his appearance was revolting, and his purple dress and the lipstick looked ridiculous, still I wanted to kiss him more than ever.

Perhaps he saw that look in my eyes, perhaps he was simply afraid that now would be the only opportunity, that I'd walk in to meet the prophet and never come back. But this time, he didn't pull away. With both of his mangled hands cradling my face, he leaned down to kiss me. And with my eyes closed in that lush green bathroom stall, I saw him as I remembered him—my handsome friend with the deep brown eyes.

Once we started, I didn't want to stop. As we tore ourselves apart, he wiped my mouth with the sleeve of his dress. Some of his lipstick had come off on me. "That's a new one," he joked.

"I have to leave, don't I?"

He nodded. "One last thing. Did you bring any of the pills we gave you?"

"Just one. It's in my shoe."

"Give it to me."

I pulled it out and handed it to him, and then I kissed my hideous friend on the cheek once more. "Thank you," I whispered in his ear.

I slipped out of the stall and looked at my reflection in the mirror. The same as ever. I couldn't believe that same face held all these new secrets.

I walked back out and joined my father. "Are you ready?" he asked.

"I'm ready."

# CHAPTER 8

We passed through the metal detectors and arrived in a waiting area stuffed to the brim with Outcasts. I saw them looking at me, judging my presence—what could I possibly need from the great Prophet Joshua? The wait seemed interminable. Even though my father told me that the prophet's associates, like Samuel, handled most of these people, and those who did see him directly did so for only a moment, I couldn't imagine that Joshua could possibly get to all these people today, much less do whatever it was that prophets do when they're not healing the damned.

A man, I assumed from his suit, sat in the row next to us, his wheezing breaths coming slower and more strained. I nudged my father, gestured to him. We both recognized it. The man was dying.

"Should we say something?" I asked.

My father hesitated a moment, then walked up to the woman at the front desk. He whispered something to her, gestured to the man. She nodded, and my father came back. He whispered, "They're going to try to move him up."

I smiled. Moments later, the receptionist called, "William!" and the man struggled to stand. My father immediately jumped to his aid, helping him toward the door, where a woman with a wheelchair was waiting.

When my father returned, I whispered, "Am I taking someone else's spot? These people look like they need help more than I do."

My father shook his head. "You do need it right now, even if you don't look it."

I nodded, watching a woman across the room slump in her seat. Was she breathing? By helping that man, had we killed that woman? I pointed her out to my father, but before we could do anything, we heard "Grace?"

I rose. To my father, I said, "Are you sure someone else shouldn't . . ."

"This spot is yours. You deserve it."

We walked toward the open door. I looked back in apology at the dying woman, now unconscious. "Will someone help her?" I asked.

But before he could answer, we landed in front of a large golden door. A man, one of Joshua's aides, stood outside, nodded a greeting to both of us.

"Can I take your coats and shoes?"

"Of course," my father answered for both of us. As I removed my shoes, now empty of pills, I was so relieved Jude found me in time.

"Namaste," the man said, walking off with our belongings.

My father squeezed my hand, knowing I needed the encouragement. As difficult as it was to be around him, forced to hold in all these secrets, I was grateful to have my dad there with me for this. The golden door opened, and we stepped into the prophet's chambers.

As we entered, Samuel gave my father only the most polite and cursory nod. He was a small man—sweaty, with little eyes that flicked back and forth anxiously. His face held no trace of a Punishment, but he was certainly less blindingly attractive than someone like Prophet Joshua. Instinctively, I judged him, wondering if he deserved such a prominent position, given his appearance . . . before remembering that appearance didn't mean what I'd always thought it did. His voice oozed smarm. "Thank you for coming."

"Thank you for seeing us," my father said. I glanced at a pitcher of water on a side table, but Samuel didn't offer us any.

"I was just speaking to the great prophet. He worries about the times we live in. I've been telling him for years that world peace can't last, that the devil's out there. At last, I think he's coming around."

"I didn't realize you had such influence on his message," my father said, holding back a smile.

Samuel smiled back, aware of the dig. "I offer my counsel as is appropriate. I know you do the same." Samuel turned to me. "So you're Grace."

"Yes," I said, grateful for an easy first question.

"Your dad came to me with quite the story."

"I just told him what I saw," I said.

"So this boy. Who is he?"

I gave him a quick, innocent summary of our history. Our meeting. Our date. When I told him about the jacket, Samuel had a lot of questions. Was I sure he hadn't paid for it? Perhaps he had an account with the store, or perhaps his family owned it, too. When I got to the near rape, Samuel gave far fewer possible excuses, which I appreciated. But then he got to the most difficult question. "What about you? I hear you have this ability now?"

"Maybe. I don't know."

"Go on, demonstrate it."

I looked at my father, who gestured to me. I took a deep breath, and said, "Hell!" My face did not change.

Samuel chuckled. "You can try a little harder than that."

I said a more vile expletive, and then another, nervously watching Samuel's face. He seemed thoughtful, neither particularly shocked nor horrified.

"Well?" my father asked, nervously.

"You know, sometimes it has to do with growing up. Adults are often Punished less for swearing than children."

This seemed to be new information to my father. "What about this boy?" he asked. "He did much worse things. It can't be a coincidence."

"Probably not."

I held my breath. Samuel was staring at me, trying to puzzle me out. "Have you done anything else?" he asked.

"Not really," I said. Then, after a look from my father, I said, "I went to the black market."

"Black market?" Samuel was intrigued.

"It was this place Ciaran showed me. But that's not bad, is it? I didn't think it was a bad place to go, if you didn't buy anything." *I don't feel guilty*, I was trying to tell him. *If you know how this system works, you shouldn't assume I'm lying.*

"Where is this place?" Samuel asked.

I told him, and then asked, "So am I sick? Is something wrong?"

Samuel smiled, laughed me off. "I don't know if you're sick—I'm not a doctor. But no, I think you're a perfectly normal, pious seventeen-year-old girl."

I smiled, relieved. "Thank you."

"You're sure she doesn't need to meet with Prophet Joshua? Just to be sure?" my father asked.

Samuel laughed, a bit condescending. "I think the prophet has more important things to deal with." I was so relieved. "Goodbye, Grace. I'll see you soon." It didn't sound menacing at the time—I left feeling elated, free. But now, thinking back, those words echo in my head with more foreboding . . . because I know what came next.

# CHAPTER 10

'd managed to keep my nerves in check until the moment we stepped out of Samuel's office, but walking down the mirrored exit hallway, I was visibly shaking. Outside Walden Manor, I looked around for a motorcyclist in a blue helmet, but all I saw were crowds of pious tourists snapping pictures of the building. Jude must have left while we were in the waiting room.

When we got home, my father went up to his study. Our day had inspired next Sunday's sermon, it seemed. I took a deep breath, alone in the kitchen. For the first time since that date with Ciaran, I felt safe.

Safe, but alone. I could still feel that kiss hovering on my lips, that strange, ugly, magical kiss in the bathroom with Jude. I was antsy. I couldn't focus on anything. Every book I read, TV show I watched—the stories felt hollow. It all seemed so fake, all these people going about their lives with no idea that everything they believed in was a lie. Every class I attended the next day was full of people who felt just as fake. It was alienating. Like living in a whole other country, on a whole other planet, from every single person I interacted with.

I sat in history class, tried to focus on the teacher's words, but even history, a subject entirely devoted to facts, was full of fiction. A whole made-up story of how our world came to be. Macy was still out sick, and I was tasked with collecting her homework, which meant heading to her house and risking an interaction with Zack. The prospect terrified me. I was afraid my midnight phone call to him might have outed me, and I wanted to stay as far away from him as possible.

As I walked home from school, I knew I had to go to Macy's. But instead I walked aimlessly. Down streets that led far from her house, far from anywhere I'd ever been before. The unfamiliarity felt refreshing somehow—that perhaps outside of my insular circle of acquaintances, I could find someone who knew the truth, someone I could talk to.

And perhaps Jude would find me. That was the real reason for my wandering, though I couldn't have articulated that at the time. He'd been watching me before, so perhaps he still was, perhaps fate would lead me around a corner and I'd find him, waiting for me. I kept an eye on the cars whizzing by, on the pedestrians I crossed paths with. He had to be around here somewhere. And indeed, out of the corner of my eye, I'd occasionally catch a glimpse of what looked like the same car, driving behind me, street after street. Then again, there were a thousand black sedans on the road, so who could say if it was the same one? But deep down I hoped it was Jude.

Maybe all I had to do was find somewhere secluded, somewhere no one would see us. We could carry out a whole relationship in dark alleys until this war was over. I walked without thinking through dim, unlit streets, the kind I wasn't trained to be afraid of, having been raised in a crime-free world. I leaned against a grimy brick wall and closed my eyes, hoping that when I opened them, I'd see Jude.

In the darkness behind my eyelids, I heard a faint noise. Footsteps. I opened my eyes, but saw no one.

And then a shadowy figure grabbed me. Put a rag over my mouth, as I struggled against his grasp.

And as I fell to the ground, just before I lost consciousness, I looked up at my attacker. It wasn't Jude. It was Clint Ramsey.

# CHAPTER 11

I woke up in a dark basement that smelled of mildew. Boxes lined the walls, a few long-abandoned children's toys peeking out of them. Through the small, high window in the corner, I could see the sun rising—I'd been passed out all night. I was alone, and my head was killing me. I tried to stand, only to realize I was tied down, expertly bound to a heavy armchair. At this point, I began to truly panic. I considered calling for help, but I wasn't sure where I was, how far from anyone who might be able to help me. I felt for my cell phone. It wasn't in my pocket anymore—who knew where it might be. If Clint had left it behind when he attacked me, no one would be able to track me here.

Clint—why on earth would Clint Ramsey be kidnapping me? My brain immediately went to the obvious. *He's an Outcast.* He'd already told me he made a lot of mistakes. *He's a bad guy.* But then I remembered "bad guy" wasn't as simple as I'd always thought it was. Even Outcasts wouldn't do things for purely evil reasons, right? And I realized—*Clint still doesn't know what happened to Ciaran.* And if he knew I'd been out with him that night . . . of course I'd fall under suspicion. I remembered seeing Clint at the black market that day, the impulse I'd had to go up and tell him the truth—why hadn't I done it? Forget my own selfish fear; it would have been the right thing to do. And now I was paying for that selfishness.

Or was I? As the minutes passed, and silence filled the house, a calm came over me—perhaps I'd been left alone. Clint was nowhere to be seen. My initial panic began to subside into more rational preparation. With enough time to formulate a plan, maybe I could escape. I saw a side door—if I could work my way out of these restraints, I guessed I could get away. I examined the twine knotted around my hands, wondered if I could make it fray with enough friction. Thorough experimentation proved that was not likely. I turned then to the chair itself—perhaps it had a weakness I could exploit. And indeed, as I used every bit of my strength to lift the chair off the ground just the tiniest bit, I could hear a scraping sound from inside. Something was broken. If I could stress that broken piece, perhaps I could dismantle whatever I was tied to, perhaps I could get an arm free.

As I struggled against the chair, I heard a noise upstairs—voices. Clint, I assumed, and a woman . . . maybe his wife, Rowena? Getting louder, coming into earshot. The woman's voice, panicked. "Just let her go, dump her on the side of the road somewhere."

"We can't do that," Clint said.

"You don't know she saw you. You knocked her out. Maybe she won't remember."

"What if she does?"

There was silence for a moment. Some murmuring. Finally, he said, "This is the only way. We'll be careful."

"She's dangerous. What if . . ."

"I'll handle this," he assured her. I wondered why they could possibly think I was dangerous. Maybe for the same reasons Dawn had—my father's connection to Prophet Joshua? But my gut said it was something else.

"Let me talk to her first." The door creaked open, and I saw female legs descending the stairs. Rowena came into view, lit only by the dim overhead lights. She shook with nerves, with anger. Staring into her face terrified me even more than staring down the prophet. I wanted to say something, but I didn't know what could possibly calm her.

Finally, she broke the silence. "Do you know who I am?"

Was there any value in playing dumb? I guessed not. "You're Ciaran's mom, right?"

"That's right. Now the question is, who are you?" Her smile reminded me so much of Ciaran's, but it was furious, unhinged.

"I'm Grace. What's going on?" I asked.

"You know I thought it was strange. Teenage girl in a care center. Cozying up to my husband, asking questions. He said I was jealous, isn't that funny? He was sure you were just who you said you were. That your innocent act was too over the top to be a fake. You showed him, huh?"

"I'm sorry, I'm confused," I said, trying to make sense of all of this.

"I know who you really are, Grace," she said. Fear shot through me—could she know about my connection to Dawn?

Did she know I knew the truth? "We don't want to hurt you. We just want to know who you're working for."

"I'm not working for anyone," I said.

"You've been following our son," she said. "You and all the others. I want to know why."

"I don't know what you're talking about."

"Yes, you do. You and your friend, the one who came by pretending to be a cop, asking lots of questions. Watching our house."

I racked my brain, trying to figure out who she was talking about. Dawn wouldn't have posed as a cop. *But Zack would have.* Zack, and whoever he was working with. *She must think I'm like them,* I realized. If Zack's whole organization was targeting Ciaran, Zack might not have been the first person to make an attempt on his life. For all I knew, the Ramseys had encountered dozens of people like Zack over the years . . . following Ciaran, until the day they finally decided to murder him. It wasn't much of a leap for them to assume I was one of those agents, too. No wonder Ciaran had kept moving schools, that he'd been so evasive . . . he'd lived his life on the run.

"I wasn't following him. Please don't hurt me."

"I don't want to hurt you," she continued, hands shaking as she lit a cigarette—another black market purchase. "Just tell us who you're working for, and why you're here."

I realized she was afraid—if she thought I was like Zack, of course she would be. I tried to keep my voice light, nonthreatening. "I'm not working for anyone. I'm a high school senior." I had no idea how to make her believe that.

"Sure you are. How old are you really?" she asked, taking a drag of her cigarette. "Twenty-four? Twenty-five? That'd put you about with the others who've been spying on us."

"I'm seventeen," I said. "I think you have me confused with—"

"You're Grace Luther. I've looked you up. Your online persona is perfect. Where is Ciaran?" she asked. I could hear the desperation now.

"I don't know," I said, a little less convincing this time.

She picked up on my hesitation. "You know something. Tell me."

"I don't."

"Tell me, and I'll let you go."

I watched Rowena shake . . . and I felt a strange kind of sympathy. I imagined what she must be going through, missing her son. She didn't know I wasn't like Zack, she didn't know I was one of the good guys. So I had to take a risk. I had to tell her the whole truth. Because she deserved it, and because it was my only way home. I had no idea what Zack might do if he learned I'd witnessed the murder in the woods, but I saw no other way out of this situation. I took a deep breath. "Ciaran is dead." I tried to ignore the horror on her face as I continued, "A man came into the woods and killed him. And took him away. I don't know why . . ."

Her eyes flashed with rage. "I don't believe you."

"It's the truth!" I insisted. For once it was. For once I wished I had *more* information rather than less, that I knew what Zack was a part of, that I could point her at his organization without getting myself into deeper trouble. "I'm so sorry," I said, "I know this must be hard for you . . ."

"My turn." Clint had stepped into the room, bottle of liquor in hand. He took a sip from the bottle, and I watched as his face slowly changed, became more attractive. He smiled. "She's a professional. She's not scared of a few questions. Let's see how she reacts under pressure."

# CHAPTER 12

I still wasn't used to being afraid of people. As Clint and Rowena closed in on me, the voice in my head still insisted, *They can't hurt you. Great Spirit will Punish them.* But I had to quiet that voice and remind myself . . . it wasn't about Great Spirit, it was about guilt. If Clint felt that he was justified in his actions, that I was a member of some evil organization that had taken his child, who knew what he might be capable of doing. I also wondered about the effects of alcohol . . . did that change the intensity of guilt one felt—was that why Clint's face changed? Until, like the pills, it wore off. Was that why it was Prohibited? Like Xanax, was it another way to change your brain chemistry, avoid Punishment? If Clint had been defending Ciaran his whole life, covering up his other near rapes, or worse . . . maybe drinking was the way he got through the morally questionable things he'd surely had to do?

Of course, all this flashed through my head in an instant of sheer terror. "Please, I've told you everything I know," I said.

"So you say our son is dead," Clint said, voice slurring a little as he took the pack of cigarettes from a wary Rowena.

"Yes," I said, "I'm so sorry . . ."

"Why didn't you call the police?"

"I did call the police," I said. "They didn't do anything."

"And you didn't think to contact us. Let us know our child was dead." Clint seemed genuinely upset about this point.

"I'm sorry, I know I should have. I was afraid. I didn't know what was happening. If the police didn't believe me, why would you?"

Clint flicked his lighter on and held a cigarette to the flame. He removed it very slowly, his eyes never straying from mine. "Tell us about this man. This murderer."

"He's not dead. She's lying," Rowena cut in.

"Let her tell us her story," Clint said. "Now, Grace—where is Ciaran?"

"He's dead," I said, my voice trembling with fear. "I'm so sorry, I should have told you . . ."

He lowered the cigarette to the inner crook of my elbow. Paused. "Are you sure? Are you sure that's what happened?"

I stared at that smoking little weapon. Saw in Clint's eyes that he meant to use it. I realized I'd made a strategic error—if they believed I was responsible for what had happened to Ciaran, and I convinced them he was dead, that made me his murderer, in their eyes. Even the most kindhearted parent would be brutal to their child's murderer. Unless I backtracked and convinced them Ciaran wasn't dead at all. I squeaked out, "I wasn't that close. I didn't see for sure. Maybe he's still alive. He could still be alive."

I looked desperately at Rowena, who was staring at Clint, brimming with renewed hope. "See?"

"He's dead, he's alive, you can't make up your mind, can you?" But I could see the hope flitting through Clint's eyes as well.

"Where is he?" Rowena asked.

"He's with that man," I said. "The one who shot at him. But I don't know . . ." I was interrupted as Clint lowered the cigarette to my arm. At first the pain just confused me—in my sheltered seventeen years, I'd never experienced pain like this before. I screamed as I heard the skin sizzle. I thrashed away as best I could, but Clint held my arm in place. I cried, I wailed.

"Shut her up," Rowena said quietly.

"No one will hear. It's fine," Clint said.

Could he be covering? Could we be close enough to other people that I could call for help? "Help me!" I shouted at the top of my lungs.

But no help arrived. Clint never lost his focus. "Now. Tell me what happened the night my son disappeared. The truth. What did you do to him?"

I knew I only had one more chance. These people—no matter how hateful their actions—they just wanted their son back. And seeing how they'd responded to that little glimmer of hope I'd just given them, I knew I had only one option. I had to convince them I knew where Ciaran was. And I had to leverage that information. If I didn't, if I just told them Zack's address, they'd kill me for sure. I had to make them see me as valuable. "You're right, I do know something. I know who has your son."

"Where is he?" Clint's grip on my arm grew tighter.

"We were on our date, and then this man came up. I guess he'd been following us. And that man took Ciaran with him. I was scared. I thought maybe that man would be coming after me. I didn't know what was happening . . ."

"Just tell us where Ciaran is, and we'll let you go," Clint said, calm.

"I'll show you."

Clint lowered the cigarette again. "If you can show us, you can tell us. Give us the address."

I began to lose hope. They'd never let me go. The only way they'd feel safe, after this, was by killing me. Torturing me for all I had, then killing me to cover their tracks. I saw Clint's face changing, getting uglier with the guilt of what he was doing, what he knew he'd have to do.

"It's not as simple as an address. Let me go, and I'll show you." But I wasn't convincing either of them. I was starting to panic.

"Don't you dare untie her," Rowena snapped at Clint.

He grabbed the cigarette from Rowena's mouth and held it over my neck. "No, please," I begged.

"Where is Ciaran?"

"I can take you there, I can take you to find him . . ." But Clint could tell I was bluffing now. "Please, please let me go . . ." As he lowered the cigarette again, I closed my eyes . . .

And then I heard a smashing sound upstairs. Footsteps pounding on the ceiling above me. "Police!" Clint dropped the cigarette, and he and Rowena exchanged terrified looks. They didn't know what was going on either.

"Run," Clint whispered, and he ran for the side door I had been contemplating as my escape, Rowena following closely behind him. As they threw it open, they found a police officer waiting on the other side. The same police force that had dismissed my earlier call was now coming to my rescue. My heart soared. Had Jude called them? I couldn't think of anyone else who could have found me. Rowena and Clint turned and tried to flee in the opposite direction, but more officers had descended the stairs.

"She's the dangerous one!" Rowena was shouting as they handcuffed her. "Don't untie her, she'll turn on you!" But they did untie me, as Rowena flew into hysterics. "You're all working together, aren't you? It's one big conspiracy, the police, everybody . . ." She struggled against the officers. It took several of them to subdue her.

One of the officers put a blanket around me and led me outside to a waiting ambulance, where an EMT examined my burns. He said they didn't look too bad, but I should go to the hospital just in case. "She'll have to do that later," a voice behind me said.

I turned—it took me a moment to place the man who'd said those words. Bald, with ice-blue eyes—he was one of the guards at Walden Manor. What was he doing here? And then I realized Jude hadn't come to my rescue—it was this stranger. But why? How had he known to find me here, unless . . . he'd been following me. The black car I'd seen on every corner—that hadn't been Jude. It was someone sent by Guru Jenkins.

The police captain came up to him, whispered a question in his ear. His response was gruff, authoritative. "Yes, yes, take them. I'll wave you in." The captain nodded in deference as the man turned to me. "Come with me, Grace."

I followed him into a black town car. Sat next to him in silence as we drove. He offered no condolences, asked no questions. "Where are we going?" I asked.

"Samuel would like to speak with you again."

# CHAPTER 13

I t all happened so fast. The police took us through the gates of Walden Manor, relishing this moment. None of them, I imagined, had ever been this close to the prophet. It was an amazing honor, a once-in-a-lifetime experience you'd tell your grandkids about. Lucky me, I'd been here twice in one day.

I saw the Ramseys up ahead of me. Clint's face was starting to return to its Punished state as the alcohol wore off. I saw the hate in his eyes.

Once we entered Walden Manor, I made an excuse and slipped into the bathroom. No Jude. No Dawn. No one but me and my reflection. I had no pills on me—good because Samuel couldn't find them, bad because I was afraid of what my face might show without them to control my appearance. I tried to calculate when I'd taken my last pill. Twelve hours, at least. Based on my week of experience with them, the effects of these pills didn't last much longer than that.

I walked through security, instinctively making a little silent prayer to Great Spirit. Though my faith had been shaken, my need for comfort remained. I just had to survive the next hour. I steadied myself. I could do this. I'd done it once before and survived. *Survived but gotten myself followed.* It was no accident that guard had found me, marshaled a whole SWAT team to rescue me. He'd been sent by Samuel to track me, I knew it. Which meant something I'd done had tipped Samuel off.

This time there was no delay. We walked right past all the dying Outcasts and straight to the golden doors. There was no one waiting to take our shoes. The door opened, and we all entered.

Samuel did not seem so welcoming this time. He carried the same air of importance, but with a harder edge. He smiled as I entered, but his focus was, mercifully, on the Ramseys, his eye acutely critical. The Ramseys themselves were humbled by his presence and immediately grew silent. For all their panic over a police conspiracy, they never imagined such evil could spread all the way to the prophet's office.

"Who are these people?" Samuel asked the guard who'd been following me.

"The parents of the boy."

"We weren't going to kill her," Clint began.

I couldn't control myself. "He burned me with a cigarette!"

Samuel raised his eyebrows. "I'd like to hear the whole story," he said. "From the beginning." His eyes bored into theirs, watched them squirm with a self-satisfied smile.

So they began. They went back and forth talking about their son, who was blessed by Great Spirit, who could do no wrong, and all the things they'd had to do to protect him from being discovered by people who might misinterpret his behavior. "People would see him do something that seemed strange—they'd catch him in a lie, they'd see him hurt someone else, and we'd find ways to help him. Lying, maybe a bribe, never anything too bad," Rowena insisted, and it took every fiber of my being not to scream out a correction. Given what I'd experienced of Ciaran, I imagined a dead girl or two might be buried out in the woods somewhere with Mommy and Daddy's help. But under Samuel's watchful eye I held my tongue.

"Did you ever confide any of this in a cleric?" Samuel asked.

"Of course," she said. "But we always got the same answers, that we were imagining things. That Great Spirit rewards good and Punishes evil. We wanted to protect our son. He's special. What were we supposed to do?" In that moment, I felt a surprising pang of sympathy for Rowena Ramsey. She loved her child deeply, and the story she told, just trying to make sense of a world she didn't understand . . . it sounded familiar. I thought of all the lies I'd told, the dangerous people I'd protected in order to save my own skin. There was nothing she'd done that I wouldn't, if I were in her place.

"Great Spirit's given you quite a test, hasn't he?" The voice wasn't Samuel's—it was deeper, and it boomed from the back of the room from a man who had entered, unnoticed, while I was engrossed in their story. As he stepped forward, I realized who he was. Prophet Joshua.

# CHAPTER 14

Joshua was nothing like I expected him to be. On TV he was this charismatic, untouchably wise leader. But his expression in that room was relaxed, genuine, familiar. I immediately felt comfortable around him, when I didn't stop to wonder what his part in this whole conspiracy might be. The only thing off-putting was his appearance—he was truly the most attractive, captivating person I'd seen in my life. The moment he walked in, the whole tenor of the room changed. We held our collective breath, and every eye was fixed on the prophet's movements.

Like a good host, Joshua poured Clint and Rowena cups of water, which they anxiously took. "Have a sip," he said. I held my breath, expecting their faces to morph dramatically. That was, I'd assumed, why Jude had told me not to eat or drink anything. Anything could be laced with drugs that would enact—or repeal—a Punishment. But neither of the Ramseys changed. It seemed that clear liquid really was just water. "Thank you, Prophet," Rowena said.

"Of course," Joshua said with a smile.

"We've tried so hard to do right by Great Spirit," Rowena said, a bit pathetically.

"And yet Great Spirit is so disappointed in you," the prophet said.

"What should we have done?" she begged. "I know we made some mistakes, but wouldn't it have been wrong to abandon our son, who needs us? We made the choice we thought Great Spirit wanted—to protect our baby boy. Our boy that Great Spirit blessed."

Her husband interrupted, "Grace said she knows where he is."

The whole room turned to me. Samuel tried to catch the prophet's eye, pass some kind of knowing glance, but the prophet ignored him—entirely focused on me. This was the moment I'd been terrified of. "I don't," I said, glad to be able to tell the truth.

The prophet walked over to me, concerned. To be the sole focus of his critical eye made me tremble. "What do you know, Grace?"

"I said someone took him away. I lied to them. I was scared," I said. I knew as I spoke, my face wasn't changing. I didn't feel the tiniest bit guilty for lying to save my skin. "Clint was torturing me. I just wanted to tell them something that would keep them from killing me."

Joshua stared at me a long moment. I had no idea what my face was doing right now. If it betrayed anything, I had no idea.

"Where did you get that story from?" Joshua asked.

"I thought if I said someone else had him, they'd have to keep me alive."

"Why couldn't they tell you were lying?" Joshua asked. A good question.

"I don't know. I was so scared, I was sure they were going to."

"She was telling the truth!" Rowena cried out.

"You just invented the story out of thin air?" Joshua asked me. I wondered—did he know the truth about what had happened in the woods that night? Maybe Zack was working for him. Maybe all these people were connected.

"I told them what I thought they wanted to hear," I said, spinning. "They kept telling me I'd been following Ciaran, that there had been others following him. I made up a story I thought they'd believe." I looked at the Ramseys, as though they could offer me help of some kind. Their wordless stares forced me to return my gaze to Joshua. "I didn't know what else to do."

Joshua finally seemed sympathetic. "I'm sorry. I can't imagine what you just went through."

I nodded, grasping on to another idea. "I think Great Spirit put the words in my mouth. I didn't even know what I was saying, I just let Him talk for me. I was praying that I could keep them from killing me, from doing any lasting damage, that someone would come and rescue me. And He sent you." I gestured to the guard with ice-blue eyes, hoping my trembling would be seen as innocent, my fear mistaken for gratitude. "Thank you," I said to him.

"You're welcome." The guard smiled back at me.

Perhaps Joshua considered the issue resolved, one way or another, because he didn't ask any more questions. He simply returned to the Ramseys, asking, "Clint, Rowena. Are you ready to experience the power of Great Spirit?"

He reached out and made contact with both of their heads. At his touch, I saw Clint's face repair itself, nearly glow. This was the prophet's famed healing touch. It was as impressive as the images I'd seen on TV, more magical in person than I could have imagined, even now that I suspected it wasn't magic at all.

"Great Spirit," Joshua began to pray, "please Forgive these two people. Their crimes might have been great, but they committed them out of love for their child. And isn't love the very thing you intend for us all to aspire to, in your name?"

The Ramseys quivered, fearing Great Spirit's reprisal. Joshua continued, "Whatever your judgment, we accept it with open hearts." As he said this, Mrs. Ramsey let out a scream. Her face began to change, morphing more dramatically, horrifically, than I'd ever seen. Clint's followed soon after. Within seconds, they were on the ground, struggling to breathe.

"No!" I screamed instinctively. Only self-preservation restrained me from rushing to their sides. As their wrists swelled beyond the width of their handcuffs, the skin split, and they began to bleed.

Joshua prayed intently. I stared at him. I was sure he'd poisoned them somehow.

While everyone's attention was focused on the Ramseys, one person had his eyes on me—Samuel. I felt my face—it was bloating, changing. I'd been so focused on the Ramseys' plight, I hadn't noticed. I realized the depth of the guilt I felt for my role in bringing the Ramseys here, that they were bleeding on the floor because of me. Because I'd been selfish, gone to the black market where Clint could see me. Because I'd listed their crimes to the prophet. Because I knew things they didn't, that as terrible as these two people were, deep down I felt like it was in some way my responsibility, with my extra knowledge, to find some way to protect them. My guilt was changing my face—I could feel it, and everyone around me could see it.

I hid my face in my hands. I took a deep breath. I'd had to do what I had to do, I told myself. I tried to harden myself to the realities of the world. I had to be more like the Ramseys. I had to see my actions as justified, and I had to do it now. And slowly, I felt the Punishment begin to reverse.

"Grace?" It was the prophet's voice. I had to look up. I removed my hands, hoping I'd healed myself in time . . . and I saw a gruesome scene before me. Both of Ciaran's parents, dead, in pools of blood. I couldn't hold back the tears in my eyes. "Sometimes the work Great Spirit has to do isn't pretty," Joshua said. "But that's the price of living in His heaven on earth."

I nodded. "I'm not used to seeing people pay that price."

His expression was grim. "You're lucky. I see it every day."

"That must be hard," I said. I couldn't believe I was standing here comforting Prophet Joshua.

He nodded morosely. "Great Spirit provides great bounties. And great pain." His eyes held a warning. My breath caught in my throat. Was the prophet threatening me? And then he smiled, the warning fading away. "I'm glad you're all right, Grace."

"Thank you, sir," I said, bowing my head in deference.

Joshua turned, leaving the room. Samuel was supervising two of Joshua's aides, who'd entered to collect the Ramseys' bodies. The guard nodded to the exit door, and he accompanied me out into the mirrored hallway. I was relieved to see that my appearance seemed to be normal. I had survived.

When we exited the building, my father was standing, waiting for me. Someone must have filled him in on how I got here, because he shook as he hugged me. "Thank Great Spirit, I was so worried." I held him in that hug as long as I could. I'd never been happier to see my father.

"They're dead," I told him. "The Ramseys."

He nodded, somber. "Great Spirit's work is done."

It wasn't Great Spirit, I wanted to tell him. It was Joshua, or Samuel, I'm sure of that. But I held my tongue as we drove home, again. It was over. I hoped now, maybe, I could go back to my regular life. As back as you can after causing the deaths of two people and having your entire worldview smashed to bits.

Or maybe I wouldn't need to. Because as we pulled into our driveway, I saw a familiar motorcycle waiting outside. Jude. As we pulled up, he drove away, around the corner. I turned to my dad. "Can I borrow your car to run to the store? I'm dying for some ice cream."

I was done with all of this. Every relationship I had from now on would be full of lies. Everything I'd ever cared about was gone, and I'd never get it back. I only had one honest thing left, and it was Jude. I had to find a way to keep him. Even if it meant giving up everything else.

I was going into hiding with Jude.

# CHAPTER 15

I followed his motorcycle for block after block, mile after mile. He finally pulled off the road outside a ramshackle village—an Outcast encampment, it looked like. As he pulled off his helmet, I could tell he wasn't happy. "What are you doing here?"

"I came to see you."

"You shouldn't follow me like that. I told you, I can't see you anymore."

The way he spoke made me angry. "I almost died today. Twice. But instead, I watched two other people suffocate and bleed in front of me. And there was nothing I could do to stop it."

"I'm sorry," Jude said, his tone shifting.

"I want to leave, I want to get out of here. I want to disappear like you did."

"That's not so easy," Jude said. "Dawn had to get a lot of people to help me . . ."

"I don't want her help. I want yours."

"I can't help you, Grace."

"Yes, you can. We can just leave, we can just run away to some other country where no one knows us and start over."

He was suddenly tense, his expression drawn in sharp lines. He said, as gently as he could, "What makes you think I'd want to do that?" The statement hacked me right through the heart.

Thrown, I tried to explain, "Because you can't be with anyone you love either. But if I went with you . . ."

"I don't *love* you, Grace." He said it gently, but firmly.

"What do you mean?"

"You're my friend. I care about you, of course. But we're very different. Even if the accident hadn't happened . . . I remember what I was thinking, right before we crashed. You'd put me on the spot. I was trying to figure out how to let you down without hurting you. Because I didn't want to lose you as a friend."

I tried to wrap my mind around this, make it make sense. "But the kiss . . ."

"In the bathroom? You were walking into a dangerous situation. I wanted to give you courage, make you feel loved."

"Even though you don't love me."

"As a friend, of course I do. But I have another life, I have other responsibilities."

"And they're more important than me?"

"A lot of things are more important than you, Grace!" He was frustrated, angry now. I'd never even considered—did he have a girlfriend out there somewhere? His next sentence, though he said it as gently as he could, cut through me like a steel blade. "I've never been in love with you and I never will be."

"But you've been following me . . ."

"To save your life. That was how I convinced Dawn not to shoot you—I said I'd keep an eye on you, make sure you didn't put us in danger." It made sense. It all made sense.

So that was it. He didn't love me. One more brutal truth. One more thing that had been staring me right in the face my whole life that I was too stupid and self-involved to realize. I looked at him for a long time. "If that's how you feel, that's how you feel," I said.

"I'm sorry," he said, full of compassion. Even now, when he was breaking my heart, he was still the best guy I'd ever met. I tried my best not to burst into tears.

"You're a good friend," I said. "I won't bring it up again."

Tentatively, I reached out and took his hand, squeezed it. Mercifully, he let me. "Are you going to be okay?"

I tried to imagine a time when I might be, and came up short. "Yeah," I lied.

He looked at me with sympathy. "I know you will be." He let go of my hand, and I walked back to my car. I waited until he'd walked out of sight, into the camp, and then I sat in my car and began to sob.

# CHAPTER 16

I cried and cried and cried. I wasn't sure why I'd been surprised. The past week had been one moment after another that proved just how little I knew about anything. The world wasn't what I thought it was. Jude was alive. Jude didn't love me, had never loved me. Everything I thought I knew for certain, in my shallow little brain, was just dead wrong. I was a stupid, stupid little child, and I was getting exactly what I deserved for all of my self-satisfaction, my smugness.

All I wanted to do was wallow in my heartbreak, and in the guilt I felt over Clint and Rowena. As soon as I got home, I bolted for my room, ready to take a pill, the kind that would at least mute the loud hammering of remorse inside my brain. If I couldn't leave town, I was going to hide from my father and the rest of the world as long as I could.

But as I opened my bedroom door, my adrenaline jolted. Someone was sitting on my bed. And it wasn't Jude. It was Zack.

Before I could scream, he grabbed me and put his hand over my mouth, closing the door behind me.

I tried to stomp my feet, make noise my father might hear, but my feet made no sound on the carpet.

In one swift movement, Zack picked me up, set me on my bed, and put a finger to his lips. I stared at him, silenced. He whispered, "You can trust me. Promise me you won't scream."

I nodded, and he let go of me.

"I'm sorry to scare you like that."

"What are you doing here?" I asked him.

As he prepared his response I realized how upset he was. Vulnerable even. "I need your help," he said finally. "It's Macy. She's dying."

# BOOK
## FOUR

# CHAPTER 1

Why? How?" I asked.

"Did you tell her about the pills?"

The way he looked at me, with such urgency, it was hard to lie. But I tried. "What pills?"

"The ones you stole from me. Does Macy know about them?"

I feigned frustration, loudly saying, "I don't know what you're talking about." Zack clamped a hand back over my mouth and put a finger to his lips again. I just stared at him, shaking with fear.

"I'm not going to hurt you. I need your help. *Does she know what you know?*"

He eased his hand away from my face, and I squeaked out, "No." Zack sighed and sat down on the bed next to me. "Why?"

"I messed up."

"How?"

"I knew it was you. I should have . . ." As Zack tortured himself with this new knowledge, I looked at the door. I wanted to run, but I was afraid of Zack catching me. "Have you told anyone else about them?"

"No."

"Did Ciaran take you home after your date?"

"Yes." Zack looked at me a long moment. I could tell I hadn't fooled him, so I said flatly, "No, he didn't."

"Then I guess you already know that I don't have a boring office job," Zack said. I nodded. "And you can probably guess that I can't tell you anything about it."

"If you can't tell me I can't guess."

"If you promise to stay quiet about this, and if you help me save Macy, I can keep you safe. Not from everyone, and not forever, but from the people I work for." A shiver ran down my spine. How many more people like Zack could be out there?

I asked again, "What happened to Macy?"

He hesitated. And then he told me.

# CHAPTER 2

He said he should have suspected me as the pill thief. But if it had been me, that would have left too many loose ends. It would have meant I'd probably seen him in the woods, which would have compromised his position at work (I didn't ask what that meant). So he convinced himself it couldn't have been me, that I hadn't had access, that he would have been able to tell immediately if I'd stolen from him.

And in fact, he'd noticed Macy had been extra beautiful lately. He wondered, had she found the pills? He tried to ask her, but he was met with Macy's usual snark. "Gross. Why would I go in your room?"

Zack called a friend from his team and explained the situation. "I don't think she's doing it maliciously. I doubt she knows anything. For all I know she just started using a new moisturizer that's making her skin look great." I happened to know that was exactly what had happened—a moisturizer I'd recommended.

Zack's friend was understanding. "You wouldn't be the first

to be careless with your meds. You just need to test her. If it turns out she's found them, we have a protocol."

"How do I test her?"

His answer didn't surprise me. It would involve the kind of pill Jude had taken when he met me in the Walden Manor bathroom. "Give her half of that, mix it in with her food so she doesn't know she's taking it, and if she's not on uppers, she'll react to it. If she is, nothing will happen, and you'll know we need to bring her in."

Zack did as he was told. He mixed the powder from the pill into Macy's mashed potatoes. An hour later when she was still on the couch, seemingly fine, refusing to give him the remote—that seemed to resolve that question. Zack debated what to do. His friend hadn't told him what exactly the "protocol" was, but Zack knew enough about the organization he worked for to be wary of what might happen to his sister if he followed orders.

He decided maybe he should just talk to her. See if he could convince her that the pills were harmless and get her to give them back. He waited until their parents had gone to bed and then knocked on her door.

"Macy?" She didn't answer. He knocked again. Still nothing. The door was locked.

He knocked on his parents' bedroom door. "Mom, have you seen Macy?"

His mom was annoyed, sleepy. "Isn't she in her room?"

They both went down the hall. "Do you think something happened?" Zack asked, worried. For all he knew, the pill was poison. Maybe that was "protocol."

"I'm sure it's fine," Mrs. Cannon said. "Macy, I'm coming in!"

She jiggled the knob. "Macy, open the door!" Still no response. "We're going to break it down if you don't open it."

"I'll get a crowbar." Zack ran down to the garage, frantic. Had he just killed his sister?

His hands shook as he tore through his father's toolbox, pulled out anything that looked like it could break down a door. He ran back upstairs. Macy's door was open now. He cautiously approached her room. Macy was sitting on her bed, crying. Her skin was crusty, her eyes yellow. She looked ill. He knew for certain that she hadn't been on "uppers" . . . this was the kind of Punishment that all the makeup in the world couldn't fix.

Her gruesome face, scrunched with tears, choked out, "I don't know what I did!"

Their mother held her and waved a hand to shoo away Zack. "Is there anything I can . . ."

"Close the door," Mrs. Cannon said, terse.

Her motherly instincts were heightened. She quarantined the room, forbade outside contact. It turns out this was Macy's "flu," which I'd been too distracted by my own problems to think much of. Zack waited anxiously in his room . . . surely this new pill would wear off after a few hours, like the others did. But he hadn't counted on the psychology of it. He didn't know as I did that the pills affected guilt. So as Macy continued to feel guilty for her imaginary crimes, her appearance remained the same. Worsened even.

Zack called his associate and explained the situation. "Don't worry," the friend said. "That happens sometimes. It's a weird side effect. Feed her the regular pills for a couple days and she should be fine."

So he tried. He made her favorite chocolate milkshake, laced with the life-saving drug. But his mother's quarantine was airtight, specifically as it related to Zack. "Macy says she doesn't know what caused this, but I do. I see how the two of you interact. Your sibling squabbles are the root of all of this," she said to Zack. "The way you two talk to each other. This bickering, it's childish, and now that you're adults, clearly Great Spirit disapproves."

"Then let me in there to patch things up, please." He held out the milkshake.

"It's too risky right now," his mother said. "One more Punishment could send her over the edge. My daughter's already an Outcast, I couldn't bear it if . . ." She couldn't say the words.

"Then please just give her this." He practically shoved the shake at her.

"All that sugar is the last thing she needs right now."

He tried desperately to sneak the pill into something else, but Macy had stopped being able to swallow. His mother called a doctor, hoping to put her on IV fluids at home. She couldn't bear to risk the embarrassment to the family if Macy was seen by the outside world. But when the doctor saw Macy's condition, he insisted she be put on twenty-four-hour care at a hospital. The Cannons gave an order to hospital staff—Zack was not permitted to see her under any circumstances. He tried valiantly, even tried to push his way through the orderlies, before he was escorted out by security.

Furious and terrified, he called his friend again. "You have to do something. You can't just let my sister die."

"We'll see what we can do," the man said. "I've passed it up the chain. I should have a response soon."

Another day passed, with no word, no help. Which was when Zack thought back on my mysterious midnight phone call and figured out who the real culprit was. And he came to me.

"You're the only one left who can help her," he said.

I didn't know if it was a trick. And after coming so close to being free, being safe, I didn't want to involve myself in anything else that might incriminate me. But I'd also caused the deaths of two people that day. And even though I no longer lived in a world where murderers were struck down by Great Spirit, even though I knew I had a pill I could take that would protect me and make me feel better . . . no pill could suppress my conscience completely. There was no pill that would ever make me a person who could sit back and let her best friend die.

"What do I have to do?" I asked.

# CHAPTER 3

I waited until I heard my father snoring before I snuck Zack back downstairs.

"I'll have you home before your father wakes up, I promise."

"That's not what I'm worried about," I said.

We drove to the hospital. It was odd . . . a couple of weeks ago I would have been thrilled to be riding in Zack's car. But now the sight of him made me sick. I'd seen him kill another human being. No matter what protection he might have promised me, this Zack, the murderer, was a stranger. I had to be prepared for anything once we saved Macy.

If we did. Zack told me her condition wasn't good. The one doctor he'd been able to corner had confided that Macy might not make it through the night. We had precious little time to get that pill in her system.

We arrived at the hospital around 2 A.M., and only one nurse was on duty at the desk. Zack hung back as I approached her—he'd already antagonized the hospital staff enough, associating with him could only hurt my case. "I'd like to see Macy Cannon. What room is she in?"

"I'm sorry," the nurse said, "visiting hours are over for non—family members."

"But I'm family!" I said. My face must have shown a trace of Punishment, guilt at the lie, despite myself, because the nurse was not swayed. I tried again. "I came all this way to see her, please, just five minutes."

"I'm sorry, it's hospital policy."

I began to cry. I think in my head they were supposed to be manipulative tears, like when you used to see women cry in movies to get what they wanted, but after everything, after the prophet, the Ramseys, Jude, Ciaran . . . one more tiny obstacle was unbearable to me. As my tears poured out, the nurse was sympathetic. "You can see her tomorrow, 10 A.M."

"What if she doesn't live until then?"

"There's no reason to think that."

"She's dying!" I said, losing the ability to control my voice. "The doctor said she might not make it through the night."

She was used to emotional people. "I understand that you're upset. But as long as you remain calm, you'll be allowed to see her tomorrow."

"I'll only be five minutes. Please." She was unconvinced. "My father is the cleric at the Tutelo Valley Worship Center. I've been praying over sick people all my life. I know I can help, I know I can save her."

"You can pray out here."

"It's not the same. Prayers are more powerful when you can be with the person you're praying for. You must know that, you must have seen that. Please just let me go in and see my friend for five minutes. If she dies tonight, I'll never forgive myself."

I saw the woman's face twinge—she felt a tiny bit of guilt. But guilt she couldn't resolve. She didn't know if disobeying the rules was worse than letting a young girl remain in distress. "Let me go talk to someone," she said.

A moment later, she returned with an older gentleman, her supervisor. "I'm sorry," he began, "but the rules say . . ."

I interrupted, "Really? You're going to let my best friend die because you're worried Great Spirit will Punish you for violating protocol?"

Their faces twinged even further. The nurse looked to the man. He sighed. "Let me talk to someone higher up."

I realized they'd just keep passing the buck to avoid taking responsibility. I could cry at these people all night, and I still wouldn't get to see Macy for another twelve hours. I returned to Zack. "Do you think she'll survive till the morning?"

"I don't know."

"Did that doctor give you any odds?"

"No, I told you everything he said." To see the normally stoic Zack this upset concerned me. "My parents are in there with her now. I could call them . . ."

"No," I said. "What if they forbid me to come in, like you? Then I won't even be able to see her tomorrow." I thought of something. "Give me the other half of that pill."

"What?"

"The bad pill. Just give it to me."

"It won't affect you, will it?" Meaning, he assumed I was taking his pills still. Was this his test? Maybe Macy wasn't in the hospital . . . maybe he just wanted to know if I'd taken the pills myself. I thought about it—I'd been Punished plenty since I took my last pill. Whatever was left in my system would be minuscule, trace amounts . . . Not knowing much about pharmacological half-lives, I had to take the risk. I shook my head. "It'll work. Give it to me." I hoped I was right, and I wasn't about to incriminate myself for no good reason. He handed it to me. I swallowed. And waited.

# CHAPTER 4

As Zack had suggested, this pill worked much more slowly than the ones I'd stolen from him. I sat next to him, nearly falling asleep. Another hospital administrator did in fact come out and tell me I couldn't see Macy. I nodded, unsurprised, and didn't put up a fight.

After an hour, I started to worry. Maybe the upper drug was still in my system.

"How long did it take Macy to be Punished?"

"About this long," Zack said. But he didn't accuse me of lying. He was kind, kinder than I expected. "I can take you home. We can come back in the morning."

I shook my head. I was determined that this would work. "I'll stay here until they let me in."

I read a magazine, some trash about how to make your godliness shine through with the right eye shadow. After reading it six times and absorbing it zero, I glanced back over at Zack. His eyes were closed. He was snoring lightly. I could get away, if I wanted to. Take Zack's car. Even without Jude, the idea of going on the run sounded appealing. It wasn't such a bad plan, really. It would solve so many problems for so many people.

Except Macy. I had to save Macy.

My own eyelids were growing heavy. Maybe if I closed them for just a second . . .

I must have fallen asleep, because the next thing I remember, I was lying with my head on Zack's shoulder. I jerked up, clutching my throat. An all-too-familiar feeling. My movement woke Zack—he took one look at me and took my hand.

"Can you stand?" I tried to, but immediately fell. "Hold on to me," he said. He put my hands around his waist, his arms around mine, and he supported me over to the nurse's station. The nurse gasped as she looked at me.

"This girl doesn't look so good," Zack said, a note of concern in his voice. He was a good actor.

"How long has she been like this?"

"I don't know. I just woke up and saw her."

"Does she have private insurance?"

"I don't know. Why would she need private insurance?"

"Punishment isn't covered by the national plan. Without private insurance, we can only take her in for one night and give her some fluids, then we have to discharge her."

"That's fine," Zack said, relieved.

"Tell her to have a seat. We'll be right with her." The way she spoke—so unfeeling, so derogatory. The way I'd always felt about Outcasts, before I knew what they really were.

Zack placed me in a seat near the window. He whispered in my ear, "Room 455." I nodded. He placed two pills in my hand, familiar and yellow. Both "uppers." I nodded again, plan in motion.

A few minutes later, a nurse wheeled out a stretcher, and an orderly helped her lift me onto it. She slipped an ID bracelet onto my wrist and wheeled me into the emergency room.

The crowded ward whizzed past me. Coughing and moaning, whirring machines steadily keeping people alive. "Keep your head down, sweetheart. We're taking you to a special place."

The Outcast Ward. I'd heard of it. That was what they always said about Jude, after he "died"—he was so sick, they didn't even take him to the Outcast Ward. Just straight to the morgue. Though in reality I guess he'd gone to neither. I wondered where that story had come from, which of Dawn's associates had spread it as a cover.

The nurse loaded me into the elevator and pushed the fourth-floor button. She was taking me straight to Macy. As we exited, the view was jarring. I wasn't sure where room 455 could possibly be . . . all I saw were rows and rows of beds. Breathing tubes and feeding tubes and the cacophonous sound of labored breathing. Hundreds of bodies stretching from one wall to the other. The nurse wheeled me through . . . I didn't know where there could possibly be an empty bed, but she found one. She and another nurse loaded me onto it. "The doctor will be right with you."

I fingered the upper pill in my pocket. Could I take it without being seen? But then the doctor approached, and I had no choice but to lie back. "How are you feeling?" he asked, rote.

"Okay," I said, voice hoarse.

"We're going to put you on some fluids. That should help."

"I'm feeling a little better," I said.

"Hopefully you'll be all better tomorrow morning. A nurse will be right back to get you those fluids."

He walked off. I grabbed for the pill again, but the nurse was on her way back with a long, thick needle. She took my arm. "This will hurt a little. Blood vessels constrict during Punishment, so it's gonna take me a minute to find a good vein, okay?"

After fifteen minutes of poking torture, she got the needle into my vein and walked away. I was left alone in a sea of bodies, Outcasts dying all around me. But I didn't have time to worry about them. I needed to find Macy. I looked around . . . the number on my bed said 217. A quick glance around told me that the numbers went higher behind me. I saw the nurses were occupied, talking at their posts many beds away. I cringed as I slipped the IV needle out and put pressure on my arm to stop the bleeding.

I stepped out of bed and dropped to the floor. I had plenty of strength to crawl, and I thought my Outcast disguise might be helpful.

The numbers on the beds grew higher, but as I reached the wall, I began to despair. The beds stopped in the three hundreds. What was I supposed to do now?

*There must be some private area*, I thought. *Maybe somewhere for people with money?* I imagined people like Macy's family would pay to keep their loved ones hidden away during a time like this. I saw a hallway to my right and headed for it.

I was certain someone would see me, this Outcast out of place, but no one noticed. Maybe no one cared. This hallway was full of rooms in the four hundreds, and as I approached 455, I saw Macy's parents sleeping inside, curled up on uncomfortable hospital chairs. Keeping a vigil next to their dying daughter. I'd made it!

I reached up and turned the door handle as quietly as possible. The Cannons remained sound asleep. I inched toward the bed, a pill in my hand. Macy was hooked up to more equipment than the Outcasts I'd seen outside. Something was making her heart beat for her. She really was dying. But I just had to get that pill under her tongue, and that would save her.

It was harder than it seemed. Crawling was easy enough, but in my weakened state, her bed was a formidable obstacle. I grabbed onto the side of it, pulled myself up. So close to my goal. But then—SMACK—I hit a button, which sent the bed electronically adjusting down.

The movement woke my sleeping friend, who cried out. Her parents stirred, startled by the sound. Seeing me in the room, some strange Outcast woman, they started screaming.

I didn't give up. I had to get that pill to Macy, no matter what might happen to me. I desperately reached for her mouth, but her father roughly pulled me away. I had no strength to fight him off. "Stay away from her!" I collapsed on the floor, my limbs bruising on the linoleum.

"Doctor! Someone!" Macy's mother ran out into the hallway, screaming, "There's an Outcast in our daughter's room!"

I had no choice. I put the pill in my own mouth and crawled out into the hallway. I'd done nothing to save Macy, and now I was trapped.

# CHAPTER 5

I pulled open a closet door and hid. I could hear people outside.

"What did this person look like?"

"Like an Outcast!"

"Male or female? Height? Build? Clothing?"

"I don't remember! It was crawling on the ground attacking my daughter. Isn't there any security here?"

The voices disappeared. I could feel my strength returning. I had to get back down to the waiting room. If they hadn't recognized me, I could blend in, as long as the Cannons didn't remember my generic T-shirt and jeans. I snuck a peek outside—I saw a few people patrolling the halls. I felt my face—I had to hope I looked different enough to escape.

I slipped out, working my way through the giant room of Outcasts, my head down, arms crossed to cover my hospital intake bracelet. A few nurses glanced my way, but no one stopped me— none of them recognized me. I knew I had to get out quickly, but

I still had one extra pill in my pocket, and I didn't want a nurse to catch me with it. I saw a young girl, a teenager, struggling to breathe in a bed up ahead. As I passed, I quickly slipped the pill between her lips. She looked at me, confused, terrified, and I didn't wait to see the results. I reached the elevator, pushed the button, hoping to avoid catching the Cannons' eyes.

The elevator came, and I stepped inside . . . along with the doctor who'd examined me earlier. He gave me a cursory nod, then looked down at his clipboard.

"You here visiting family?"

"Mmm-hmm." I was afraid he'd recognize my voice.

"Sorry to hear that," he said. "Rough night. Outcast Ward is packed."

"Mmm." His eyes flicked up from his clipboard, and he gave me a long look. Working out who I was.

The elevator dinged and opened. I held my breath as he stepped out. He watched me as I paused, waiting for him to walk away. "Looking for the exit?" he asked. I nodded. "You should go out that way," he said helpfully. I dutifully followed his advice, which took me down a long hall toward an exit sign. When I opened it, I breathed in cool, nighttime air. Freedom.

I circled back around the building. I needed to find Zack and get out of there. When I arrived in the waiting room, he was sitting near where I'd left him.

"Zack," I hissed. "We have to go."

He shook his head and shoved his sweatshirt at me. I barely had time to put it on, disguising my outfit, before I heard, "Grace?" Mrs. Cannon was right behind me. I pulled the sleeve of the sweatshirt over my intake bracelet and hugged her.

"I heard about Macy. I'm sorry, I know you didn't want anyone to know."

"We just had the most terrifying experience . . ." She then proceeded to tell me what had happened, how Mr. Cannon was upstairs keeping watch.

When she finished, I asked, "Can I go see Macy?"

Mrs. Cannon shook her head. "Not right now. I don't think she should see anyone till she gets better."

Zack cut in, "Mom, it might help . . ."

"I don't want to have this conversation right now. I thought we told you, go home, wait there." Mrs. Cannon turned back to me. "What are you doing out here this late at night?"

"I heard about Macy and came right away."

"Where's your father?"

She was accusing me of misleading him, but I knew I could get around the question by pretending to misunderstand her. "He could come if you want him to. He can pray with her, we both can."

Mrs. Cannon paused. I'd never known the Cannons to be particularly religious, but in moments like this . . . "Would he? Do you think it would help?"

"It might be the thing that makes the difference."

She hesitated. "Tomorrow?"

"He'd be glad to, I'm sure," I said. I glanced at Zack—this was our last hope.

Mrs. Cannon headed back upstairs, and Zack and I retreated to the car. "You did good," he said as he started the engine.

"Not yet," I worried.

"Your dad . . . is he going to complicate things?"

"No. He'll distract your parents. This is good."

"Thank you for coming with me tonight." I could see the fear in his eyes.

"She'll be okay," I said, comforting.

"If she's not it's my fault," he said solemnly.

I didn't disagree, but I said honestly, "It'd be as much mine. Wouldn't it?"

He knew what I meant—if I hadn't stolen his pills, he never would have had reason to suspect Macy. But he said, "You didn't know what you were doing."

"No," I said.

He touched my shoulder—I think to comfort me, but it wasn't much comfort. I didn't want this murderer any closer than necessary. I looked away, out the window. He let go. When I looked back, his eyes were on the road.

"I'll talk to my dad tonight. He comes to pray over people all the time . . . I'm sure for Macy, he'll drop whatever he's doing."

"Your father's a good man."

"Yeah." The normalcy of our conversation lulled me. Like this was just a car ride with a friend. I'd always had trouble talking with Zack, mostly because I was too nervous to think of words around him, much less entire sentences. Funny how easy it was now that I hated his guts.

But now, I could see, he was having trouble talking to me. Nervously, he began, "I'm sorry about Ciaran. This might sound stupid, but . . . I understand, I do."

I summoned all my willpower to say, "Thanks."

"And I know you think I'm a bad guy. I'm not."

I wasn't sure what to say to that, so I just nodded. After a moment of silence, I worked up the courage to ask him, "What are you going to do when this is all over? About me?"

I saw the conflict on his face. "I don't know. Is that okay?"

"I don't really have a choice."

He looked at me intently. "I know you have no reason to trust me, but I promise I'll do everything I can to keep you from getting hurt."

*Like you promised Macy?* I wanted to ask. I had to get out of this car.

We were approaching my house, finally, so I said, "I'll see you tomorrow."

I barely waited for the car to stop before I jumped out of it. I couldn't listen to the glib words of a killer. Once we saved Macy, I was going to make sure I never talked to Zack again.

I headed into my dark house, trying to make as little noise as possible. But as I headed up the stairs . . . "Grace?"

"Hey, Dad."

"What are you doing up?" He was always going to be suspicious of me now, wasn't he?

"Macy's in the hospital," I said.

His expression changed. "Oh no."

"Tomorrow, do you think we can go and pray with her?"

"Of course."

"Visiting hours start at ten."

"What's wrong with her?"

I hesitated, but he'd find out tomorrow anyway. "She's in the Outcast Ward."

My father paused. "At least it's a straightforward cure. Don't worry. Macy will be just fine."

"I hope so."

He put his hand on my shoulder. "If she's still alive, we can save her."

I headed to bed. "We" couldn't, but I could.

# CHAPTER 6

When I awoke the next morning, I was shocked to find an elaborate breakfast spread on the counter and Mrs. Cannon sitting on our couch. She jumped up to hug me. "Grace, you have no idea what this means to us."

Mr. Cannon appeared, gave me a pat on the back. "We're so proud of you."

"What did I do?" I asked.

Mrs. Cannon was breathless. "You haven't heard? Macy's going to get the help she needs. All thanks to you."

My father entered with Zack, who looked uncomfortable in his best suit. "Did they tell you the good news?" I watched Zack for some kind of hint, but his expression was stoic.

"Macy's better?" I asked.

"Not yet," my father said.

Mrs. Cannon took my hands, gushing, "Your father told us how you met the prophet yesterday, how you really impressed him. So Paul called and spoke directly to him . . ."

"Well, I spoke to Samuel," my father corrected her humbly.

"He said Macy was your best friend, and the prophet . . ."

At this point, she choked up, and her husband stepped in to finish for her. "The prophet said that any friend of yours must be pretty special. And he was going to do everything in his power to help."

My adrenaline began to rush. "What does that mean?"

"He's going to heal her himself."

"Heal her?" I asked weakly.

"And he's coming here to do it."

"To our house?"

"Isn't that wonderful?" Mrs. Cannon said, wiping away tears.

Zack added, "Thank you so much for your help." I was sure I caught a hint of a sarcastic tone in there somewhere.

"Wonderful," I choked out. My mind swam with thoughts of the Ramseys' brutal deaths. It had felt like a warning. Like Joshua telling me what he could do if I stepped out of line. And if he had any idea that I'd been talking to Dawn or even Zack . . . I was terrified to think what Prophet Joshua's "healing" might look like. My father might believe Joshua's power was magic, but I knew it was poison. I couldn't let that happen to Macy. I didn't know why the prophet was doing this, why he'd spend his valuable time coming all the way to Tutelo. He must suspect me. I couldn't think of another explanation. I had to get Macy somewhere safe.

I thought of all the people I could call. Jude would be the best, but who knew if my little bear trick would work a second time. Or if he was even willing to talk to me after the way our last encounter had ended. Dawn might know what to do, but even if I found a way to reach her, I didn't trust her, and I didn't think she'd take kindly to me risking exposing myself, especially not to save the sister of . . . whatever Zack was.

But Zack? As much as he terrified me, he was my best shot. I just had to get him alone. If he knew what the prophet was capable of, maybe he could help me keep Macy away from him. But as I tried to corner him in the kitchen, the doorbell rang. I heard my dad opening the door, and a familiar voice. Prophet Joshua. "Now, where's Grace?"

# CHAPTER 7

Joshua entered, followed by Samuel. I could see his security detail outside.

My father shook Joshua's hand, nearly bowing. "Prophet. Thank you."

"Paul, there is no need. Great Spirit called me to this place. There is important work to be done here."

"Yes," my father said, glancing at me.

The prophet turned his attention to me. "Grace. So good to see you again."

"You, too, Prophet."

His voice was so kind, so warm. "I'm sorry we're here under such unfortunate circumstances. Where is your friend?"

"She's on her way," Mrs. Cannon said, standing at a nervous distance. "The hospital is transporting her here now."

"Then, Grace, while we're waiting, why don't you give me the tour?"

I looked at my father, who nodded encouragingly. With a glance at the still stoic Zack, I said, "Sure."

I led the prophet through each room, trying to think of interesting things to say about the objects in each one. My father and the Cannons trailed behind, lapping up Joshua's every word. Mrs. Cannon kept trying to propose philosophical and religious dilemmas, things she'd always struggled with that she hoped the prophet would answer. Mr. Cannon would politely apologize on her behalf—I noticed their bickering was not entirely unlike Macy and Zack's.

Finally, we arrived at my room. I panicked at the thought of what might be lying out. Any hints that I might know the truth? The red pills, I remembered, were safely hidden in a box of tampons . . . hopefully Joshua wasn't planning to root through my bathroom cabinet?

I opened my door, stood back as the prophet stepped inside. I blushed as he surveyed the room—my unmade bed, the dirty clothes on the floor, the mess on my dresser. "I'm sorry, no one told me you were coming," I mumbled.

"No apologies necessary."

He idly opened a drawer, glancing at me with an amused smile. I was frozen, couldn't say anything, as he picked up items from it.

"I'm so glad you didn't come to our house, Prophet. I'd be so embarrassed," Mrs. Cannon was saying.

"It would be an honor to have the prophet to our home," Mr. Cannon said through gritted teeth.

"I didn't say it wouldn't be!"

Joshua was rifling through the books on my dressers. A note-book with my school assignments. He went to the window and picked up the teddy bear lying on the floor. He tossed it around a bit. Was he going to set off the voice box, with my message to Jude on it? He squeezed it, but only static came out. A rush of relief—Jude had erased the bear after listening to the message. He was a genius.

Samuel, who'd disappeared early in the tour, came back. "The girl's downstairs."

Joshua set down the bear. As he exited into the hallway, he stared me straight in the eye. That look again, carrying a warn-ing. A challenge. This time I was sure there was only one thing that look could mean. He knew.

# CHAPTER 8

My mind raced. Was it because of the Ramseys? The way my face had changed watching them die? Or was this all in my head? Was I reading too much into one look he'd given me?

I walked downstairs, and for once I stopped dwelling on my own misfortune. There was Macy, on a stretcher, more shriveled and sickly than I'd ever seen her, kept alive only by a motley crew of medical machinery.

Joshua approached Macy. Her mother reached out and touched his hand. "Thank you so much, Prophet. We can't even begin to say how much this means to our family." As Mrs. Cannon spoke, I saw her face begin to glow—Joshua was healing her. His magical healing touch seemed to be involuntary. Perhaps just touching Joshua was enough to prompt the same feeling as prayer in people's brains. Perhaps simply being in Joshua's presence could be enough to heal Macy.

I began to hope. Maybe he was really going to save my friend. Maybe this was truly the prophet trying to help me. My father had been his faithful soldier all these years . . . why had I jumped to the conclusion that this was about me? Maybe this was my father's reward for loyalty.

Joshua leaned over Macy. "Do you understand what you did wrong?" I saw a slight, barely perceptible nod. I knew it took all her strength. "Are you ready to open yourself back up to Great Spirit?" Even as he spoke the words, I saw her begin to recover. He was easing her guilt just by being next to her. He took her hands, and the transformation began. It was rapid, breathtaking. In mere moments, she went from horrifying, near-death disfigurement to a shred of normalcy. The color returned to her cheeks, the breath to her lungs, a smile to her face. And there it was again, that look from Joshua.

Was he waiting for me to confess? I looked at my father, who was beaming with joy. At Zack, who was anxiously watching his sister. Then back at Joshua.

It was on the tip of my tongue. It was the solution. It was the end of living in fear. Whatever repercussions would result would be over and done with, and I wouldn't have to worry any more. And the prophet's aura was intoxicating. Even knowing everything I knew about him, I wanted to spill all of my secrets. Looking into his eyes, I felt like he was trying to pull it out of me.

But I remembered Jude. I remembered everything he'd risked to keep me safe. Even if he didn't love me, I still loved him. And so I kept my mouth shut. And after a moment, still staring at me, Joshua let go of Macy.

It had an instantaneous effect. Macy took a deep breath in, shocked, and her appearance stopped improving. She wasn't an Outcast, for sure, but she wasn't . . . pretty. She didn't look anything like the friend I remembered. She looked up at the prophet helplessly. "How do you feel?" he asked her.

"Better."

"Are you ready to follow the path Great Spirit has set out for you?"

"I am."

"Good."

As I pondered what had just happened between Joshua and myself, Macy's mom interjected, sobbing, "Thank you, Prophet, thank you so much."

"I help where I can. I only wish I could help more." He signaled to Samuel, walking to the exit. "Good luck, Macy."

So that was it. Macy was alive. Not totally healed, but alive. As the Cannons gathered around her, the prophet turned to me. "Grace, could you come with me for just a moment?" My heart skidded to a stop.

"Of course."

# CHAPTER 9

I followed Prophet Joshua outside with a look of faux confusion and adoration. We were alone. "What is it?" I asked.

"Aren't you going to thank me for healing your friend?"

"Yes, of course. Thank you. You have no idea how scared I was."

"I'm sure."

"She's my best friend. I don't know what I would have done if I'd lost her." All honest.

"There's nothing I enjoy more than using my powers for good." I already knew what it looked like when he used them for evil. "What would you think about doing some work for me?"

"Work?" I had no idea what that could possibly mean.

"From time to time I enlist allies to help me with some important projects. Good works in the community."

"Like volunteer work?" I asked.

"And some more sensitive issues, some that may require discretion. I'll confess to having one of my men do a little research on you. But you probably already knew that."

The guard with the ice-blue eyes. "He followed me," I said.

"I'm grateful he was able to rescue you from that horrible situation."

"Me, too."

"He also spoke to some of your friends and family, and from what they say, you're the most pious and trustworthy young woman I could recruit. So tell me—are you interested?"

No! Not in the slightest. I wanted to be as far away from Prophet Joshua as possible. But I definitely couldn't say that, so I simply said, "I don't know."

He seemed surprised by my reluctance. "What don't you know?"

"I'd love to help, I just don't know if I'm the right person."

"You're exactly the right person."

"If you think so."

He put a hand on my shoulder. There was something about his touch that felt unnatural, and against my will, I felt better, healthier—healed.

"I have a mission in mind for you. If you're interested."

"What kind of mission?"

"You're starting to see the truth now, aren't you? I can tell. The world is not as simple as we want to believe it is." I tried not to panic as he continued, "There are evil forces lurking in unexpected places."

"What do you mean?"

"Grace, I began my career as a student of religion. It was a time when studying religion was much more . . . shall we say, interesting. There was nothing you could prove, and the world was filled with infinite theories about what the universe meant. You had your animists, who believed that things like flowers and trees had feelings. You know that term, Great Spirit, was inspired by the beliefs of the Sioux—many of the religions born right here in America had an animist bent. You also had your polytheists, who believed in all kinds of warring gods. With all the chaos we used to have, it made sense, I think, to have these supernatural clashes that mirrored our own. But what about monotheism? Do you know what monotheism is?"

"One god."

"Exactly. Are you a monotheist?"

It felt like a trick question. "I think so?"

"It would make sense, wouldn't it? We've lost all the trappings of Christianity and Islam and Daoism, and we worship this one, complicated entity. Sure, it manifests as a whole pantheon of gods, Vishnu and Yahweh and all those flowers and trees, rolled into one. But Great Spirit—that's our god, isn't it?"

"Yes."

"I believe He's a good guy, don't you?"

"Of course."

"But you know there's evil left in this world. Your friend Macy and her family might not know it, but you do. You've seen it. How do you explain that?"

"I can't," I said.

"Do you believe that Great Spirit created that evil? If He's good?"

"He must have. To challenge us."

"To give you free will?"

"Yeah."

"But why would He have created the concept of evil in the first place? We all blame Eve for eating that apple, but Great Spirit created a creature capable of defying Him. Which means Great Spirit Himself must be kind of a conniving guy, huh?"

"I guess so."

"So you worship an evil god? One who enjoys toying with humanity, watching us suffer over what decision to make, who enjoys watching us torment each other?"

"I don't know." I was getting tired of this. What was he getting at?

He sensed my frustration. "So you see the dilemma. For those who know that evil still exists . . . where does it come from? The only conclusion I've been able to draw, and I know it's one that might anger some of my fellow prophets . . . there is more than one power in this world."

"The devil," I said.

"That is what Judeo-Christian traditions called it, yes. But if the devil exists, and can challenge Great Spirit . . . that stands everything we know about Great Spirit on its head. It means the deity we worship isn't all-powerful. Which means the actions you and I take are even more important."

"Why?"

"Because we are in the middle of a cosmic war. It's no coincidence the Revelations occurred recently. They were the sign of greater turmoil to come. Right now, Great Spirit is winning. But people like the Ramseys—they're the devil trying to make a comeback. And we can't let him."

"But what can I do?"

Joshua smiled. Exactly what he'd wanted me to ask. He pulled something from his pocket. A business card with no name, just a phone number. "Can I trust you?"

*No.* "Yes."

"When you're ready, call this number. Help me preserve this heaven on earth." He closed my hand over the business card. There was something about being in his presence that filled me with a sense of calm. Something that made me want to do whatever he told me. I nodded, the paper getting flexible in my damp palm. "And you know, it's best if you don't tell anyone. Great Spirit's work is best done in secret."

"'Do not let your left hand know what your right hand is doing,'" I quoted.

I could tell Joshua was impressed. "I see I've chosen well. I'll see you soon, Grace." And before I even knew what was happening, Joshua was gone.

I had just been conscripted into Prophet Joshua's army.

# CHAPTER 10

What had just happened? Was this another test? Or was I wrong from the beginning—had Joshua known nothing, had he simply stared at me while he was healing Macy not as some kind of threat, but because he was planning to recruit me?

I walked inside and found my father, who was waiting by the door, excited. "Well . . . ?"

"What?"

"How did it go?" He'd known ahead of time, I realized. The prophet had told him what he was going to ask of me.

"Joshua gave me this." I showed him the business card and confided what Joshua had just said, immediately betraying the prophet's first request. My father took the card, considered it. "What does it mean?" I asked him. "What am I going to have to do? What if I don't want to do it?"

"Great Spirit only asks of us what He knows we can handle," my father said.

I wanted to press him more, but we were interrupted as

Macy ran up and hugged me. Her appearance, despite my best attempts to look past it, gave me a sick feeling in the pit of my stomach. "I can't believe that just happened," she said. Her voice sounded different—her throat was still a little misshapen.

"I'm so glad you're okay," I said.

"I'm going to go to worship centers every day for the rest of my life," she told me. She sounded like me, a couple weeks ago. If only Joshua had chosen her as part of his army instead. I cringed at the thought that maybe he still would.

The Cannons attached themselves to my father, who relished this moment to preach Great Spirit's word to Macy. She soaked up every syllable. Unable to keep a straight face, I crept away to the kitchen, where Zack was lingering. I tried to go past him to go upstairs, but he stopped me. "You can't drug her now."

"Why would I do that?" Her face, obviously. I wanted my friend to live a full life. Get the jobs she deserved, get into the right schools. With a face like that . . .

"My friends may be watching. Macy will get better on her own, if she prays enough," Zack said.

I nodded. "I'm just glad she's okay," I repeated.

"Me, too." My hand crumpled the business card involuntarily. It wasn't fair. I didn't want any of this.

I moved upstairs, closing myself off in my room. I replayed the way Joshua had touched my cheek. Unsettling thoughts. I tried to drive them away with thoughts of Jude, but those saddened me even more.

I remembered a box of Jude's things that his mother had dropped off, almost a year ago now. Things she'd thought I might want, things that pained her too much to keep around her own house, I imagined. I'd been too depressed to look at most of them, when I thought they belonged to my dead friend. But now that they belonged to the living boy I was heartbroken over, I was seized with a sudden desire to sift through them all.

It turned out to be a masochistic instinct. The box was full of notes Jude had written me in class, items I remembered from our childhood. A time capsule of what Jude had been like before the accident, memories that once had filled me with grief, but now filled me with longing. Going through it gave me reminder after reminder of how wonderful Jude was, and how much he didn't love me.

As I waded to the bottom of the box, I saw a fuzzy object: Jude's red bear, the one that matched my blue one. It had a wear and tear that felt familiar in my hands, and in spite of myself, it made me smile. I wondered what the last thing we'd recorded into it might be—probably one of my elementary school swear words. I squeezed it. But it wasn't my five-year-old voice that came out, it was Jude's sixteen-year-old one. Before the accident, he'd recorded: "Will you go out with me?"

I had to play it three times to be sure. But those were the words. A smile spread across my face. Jude had been lying. That whole brutal conversation we'd had the night before, he'd been lying. To protect me, to protect himself, I wasn't sure. But I hadn't been crazy; he'd had feelings for me, even if it was just in his former life. For once, I'd been right about something. Maybe everything was different between us now, after so much time had passed, and after what Jude had gone through—but maybe it wasn't.

The celebration was still going on downstairs, but I bypassed it—grabbing my father's keys and driving out to the Outcast camp I'd last seen Jude walk into. Navigating by memory was difficult, but eventually I saw it: a collection of trailers, tents, and makeshift wooden shacks. Even from far away, I recognized the gaits of its inhabitants. My father had been to plenty of Outcast villages in his ministering, but I'd never set foot inside one. I'd be as out of place here as I was in the black market. But now, I had at least the tiniest bit of wisdom, enough to know that wandering in here with my face could cause a cascade of problems.

I needed a disguise, and I knew exactly how to create one. I thought of everything awful I'd ever done. I thought of all the Outcasts I'd looked down on in my naïveté. I thought of Macy, who had suffered so much because of me. Of the Ramseys. Of every unkind word I'd ever uttered, of every person I'd hurt. And lastly, of Jude—of the moments before the crash that had destroyed his life, when I'd asked him a petty, distracting question. I decided to Punish myself, to remind myself of all the reasons I deserved to feel guilty. And as I did, I felt my face change, last night's pill out of my system.

I looked in the mirror. I was no longer Grace Luther. I was someone else, an anonymous Outcast.

I got out of the car. I was going to find Jude.

# CHAPTER 11

I stepped into the camp, nervous. The other Outcasts eyed me warily. Though I looked like them, they recognized that I was new, that I was a visitor here. I couldn't distinguish between them, but they could distinguish between themselves.

As I walked, an older man cornered me. "What're you here for?"

Maybe he could help me. "I'm looking for someone named Jude."

He shook his head. "Don't know a Jude."

"Maybe he goes by another name? Motorcycle, blue helmet?"

He hesitated—clearly he knew who I meant. "Why you looking for him?" Jude was someone important here, it seemed by his tone.

"He's my friend." That was not a good enough answer. I had another idea. "Dawn sent me."

He eyed me, wary. Picked up his phone, dialed, spoke to

someone on the other end. "You expecting something from Dawn?" He described me, what I was wearing.

I could hear the other voice, muffled. The man hung up, gestured down the street. I walked to where he pointed, one of these ramshackle cabins, and I knocked on the front door, a discarded piece of metal siding.

A young woman answered. She had flawless skin, and her outfit signified she was Hindu, I think. She was pretty—at least, pretty for this place. Normal. A teenager with a curious, skeptical face. She looked at me and called into the house. "Ben?"

An alias, it seemed, since Jude came to the door. He seemed shocked to see me. "What are you doing here? I told you . . ."

I pulled the red bear out of my purse. "Your mother gave this to me."

He took it. Didn't play it, but must have remembered what it said. "That was a long time ago."

"I know. But still, you said it. You can't pretend you didn't say it." I didn't break my gaze. The other girl watched us, then went back into the house. Jude looked after her. I quickly said, "Maybe I shouldn't have come."

"No. You shouldn't have."

But I didn't walk away. "You know, you're all I have left."

"That's not true."

"It is. Who am I supposed to talk to? About anything real? Macy? My dad?"

Jude was getting upset. "Don't say things like that to me. Do you know what I would give to have one conversation with my mother? One? About anything."

"I'm sorry."

"So just go home, okay?"

"I don't want to go home. What do I have to go back to? Working for the prophet?" I quickly explained everything—Macy, Zack, the prophet's offer. "If we leave, maybe we have a chance to be happy."

"What about me? Maybe I don't want to leave, give everything up."

"You mean your girlfriend?" I asked, gesturing at the empty space the Indian girl had once occupied.

Jude looked back into the house again. "She's not my girlfriend. You know people have lives outside of dating, right?"

That hit me in the gut. He was calling me out for my shallowness, my boy craziness. It hurt because it was true. It hurt because he knew me, he'd seen me for who I really was and found me wanting. "That's not what I meant."

"Why are you here, Grace?"

"Because you lied to me. Maybe you don't feel anything for me now, but once upon a time . . . you were going to ask me out."

"I was."

"Why did you lie to me?"

"Because you don't know what you're saying, running away. That's not how this works."

"Yeah? Then how does it work? You talk to me like I'm this naïve, helpless little girl, but maybe I could be more if you respected me enough to tell me the truth. You've had years to get used to this. I've had, what, a few days? You had people, you had Dawn and Father Dennehy, you had everyone in this place. I have no one." Jude was silent. "I'm leaving. I'm leaving home, leaving

Tutelo. With or without you. Maybe I'll die. But I can't stay, I can't go back and be the prophet's pawn—I'd kill myself. If you don't want to go with me, fine. But at least respect me enough to tell me the truth."

I was acutely aware of what I must look like in my "disguise." This was not how I'd hoped to look when coming to profess my love to someone. I watched Jude's face, wondering what he was thinking, wondering if I repulsed him, wondering if my words repulsed him.

Finally, he spoke. "You're right. You deserve the truth."

I held my breath. "Which is?"

He waited a moment. Let the words marinate in his gut. And then finally said, almost in a whisper, "I've never stopped loving you."

I was so happy I started to cry. Jude took me in his arms, held me. "I love you, too," I told him.

# CHAPTER 12

The inside of Jude's house was sparsely decorated. His friend, whoever she was, excused herself, leaving the two of us alone. He made me some tea. "Are you really going away? All alone?"

"What else can I do?"

He sat next to me. The tea tasted like dirt—clearly Jude didn't have a lot of money, and his groceries were the cheapest he could find. He stirred his cup, thinking. "We should ask Dawn for help."

I shook my head. "Are you kidding? She almost killed me. She won't help me with anything." Jude shrugged—maybe he agreed. "I've done missionary work before—if I tell my father I'm going on another trip, it'll buy me time to get out of the country. I think going north will be easier. Once I get to Montreal, I can take a boat somewhere else, maybe over to Nova Scotia."

"Why Nova Scotia?"

"I've heard it's pretty." He made a face. "And I can get there by car—it's harder to track someone traveling by land. And it's isolated, not like a big city where you're more likely to run into clerics who know my dad. There are lots of tourists there. People wouldn't be suspicious of unfamiliar faces. It'd be easy to get a job working in a shop or something, I just have to get a Canadian passport that says I'm eighteen and, you know, not Grace Luther . . ."

Jude smiled. "You know, I have a friend in Rochester. I think he could make us passports."

It took me a moment to notice his use of pronoun. "'Us'?"

He paused, torn. "Maybe."

I looked around the cabin. Despite its bareness, it reminded me that Jude was this entire other person, separate from the fantasy I'd concocted of him during these years apart. Someone with a whole life I knew nothing about. A life I was trying to take him away from. "I don't want you to go just for me."

"I wouldn't."

I added, for clarity, "But I do want you to come."

"I want to go, too. But . . ." He paused for a long time.

"What?"

"I shouldn't."

I tried not to be selfish. "If that's your decision."

Jude hurriedly explained, "It's not you, it's . . . I couldn't do it to them. Dawn, the others. They saved my life, and I promised I'd help them."

"Haven't you helped them enough?" Jude's instinct to be noble made my selfishness feel that much more glaring.

"In a couple years, what have I done, really? I owe them my life. I always figured that's what I'd repay them with."

"What if we did one thing that accomplished a lifetime's worth of good deeds all at once?"

Jude laughed, a little mockingly. "Sure, yeah, let's do that."

"I'm serious!"

"Grace Luther, saving the world as efficiently as possible."

I persisted. "Come on, tell me, what would be so big, so amazing, that you'd feel like you'd paid your dues?"

"I don't know. If I knew, I would have done it already."

I thought of something. "The business card." I pulled it out.

"That thing the prophet gave you?"

"If I call this number, I'm working for him. I could be a double-agent, the thing Dawn wanted me to be in the first place, the reason she saved me. I'll do one big thing to help her cause, then we can run away."

"You really want to piss off the prophet and then try to cross an international border?"

"We'll leave before he finds out. Make a run for it."

Jude was skeptical. "So what happens when you call? Do you have any idea what you'd have to do?"

I looked at the phone number. "Let's find out."

# BOOK FIVE

# CHAPTER 1

Jude called Dawn and filled her in on our plan. She was thrilled—this had been her hope for me all along. *Don't get too excited,* I wanted to say. I wouldn't be doing this for long.

I still hadn't replaced my cell phone since the kidnapping, and I didn't want to use Jude's, so we bought a burner phone at a gas station, and I typed in the number. Then paused. "Maybe this is a bad idea," I said. "We don't know who's on the other end."

"What could happen? You're just making a phone call."

I couldn't think of any other objections, so I hit the call button. My nerves jolted as the line rang. A female voice picked up. "Hello?" Nothing else. Had I even called the right number?

"Hi," I said, voice cracking. "I got this number from . . . Joshua."

"What's your name?"

"Grace Luther."

I heard typing in the background. "Are you free on Saturday morning?"

I glanced at Jude. "Sure."

"The prophet has a package he'd like you to deliver on his behalf."

My stomach was doing somersaults. "Okay."

"I'll give you the address. You'll get the rest of the instructions once you get there."

"Okay," I said, scribbling down the address she rattled off.

"Thanks so much," she said brightly, then hung up.

I looked over at Jude.

"That was easy," he said.

I nodded, still shaking. "But what good is it going to do to drop off a package?"

"This is just the part where you get them to trust you. Once you've proven yourself, then they'll give you more important things to do."

"But what if the package is bad? What if it's a bomb or something? What if it's some kind of code? 'Package' could mean anything."

"It won't be a bomb." Jude laughed a little at my paranoia.

"How do you know?"

"Why would Prophet Joshua want to bomb something?"

"I don't know. Why would he want to do anything? I have no idea what I'm walking into. If Joshua's bad, maybe this thing I'm going to do is bad."

Jude saw that I was starting to spin out. "It's going to be fine," he reassured me. "I'll follow you, I'll be right there. Whatever it is, we can handle it."

"You promise?"

"I promise." I was still shaking with fear—he wrapped his

arms around me. "You're doing a really brave thing." His praise was all the encouragement I needed.

The week flew by in a haze of dread. When Saturday arrived, I downed a pill, not willing to risk any potential guilt showing on my face, and I headed out. The appointed meeting spot turned out to be a pharmacy in the middle of town. I looked around the store. These all looked like regular shoppers. I had no idea who I was supposed to meet.

Long, uncomfortable minutes passed. Was I in the wrong place? I was about to call the number on the business card again, to ask what I was doing wrong, when a pharmacy clerk approached me. "Are you Grace?" I nodded, and she handed me a plastic bag with something heavy inside. "The address is on the box inside."

I nodded, taking it, and headed out of the store as quickly as I could. Once I was safely at my car, I took a deep breath and unloaded the bag—a box of chocolates. Innocent enough. But something didn't feel right.

I thought of the water in the prophet's office, which I could only assume had contained the poison that killed Clint and Rowena Ramsey. My stomach curdled. There was only one reason Prophet Joshua would ask me to deliver something like this— why he wouldn't simply ship it through the mail, or use an external delivery service. He needed secrecy because the chocolates were poison. I was about to commit murder.

# CHAPTER 2

Where was Jude? I drove out of the parking lot as slowly as I could, cars honking and swerving around me. This was supposed to be our signal that something was wrong. Why wasn't he pulling up next to me, why didn't I see him anywhere on the road?

My mind began to whirl. What if this whole thing had been a setup somehow? What if Jude had been tasked with recruiting me from the very beginning? What if his affection was a ploy to get me to this very moment—what if the recording in the bear I got from his mother had been a setup?

I pulled inside a parking garage to regain my composure. It seemed Jude wasn't coming to meet me, so I'd have to come up with my own plan. I had two choices: (1) try to skip town and cross the border into Canada on my own, with no time to prepare, or (2) go through with what was very likely tantamount to murder. As I struggled to think of any kind of third option, someone rapped on my window. Someone in a blue motorcycle helmet. Jude was still on my side after all.

I rolled down my window. "Where have you been?" I couldn't contain the frustration in my voice.

Jude flipped up his helmet's visor. "I'm right here. What's going on?"

"It's chocolates. The package is chocolates."

I could see Jude jumping to the same conclusion I had. "Are they wrapped?"

I showed him the box, sealed in plastic wrap. "They could have sealed them even if they're poison."

Jude examined the wrapping. "It looks like any store-bought box."

"But what if it's not? I'm not going to kill someone, I can't do it."

"Calm down. Take a breath."

I did, but against my will. "What am I going to do?"

Jude was calm, focused. "I'll go buy another box. One we know isn't poison. We'll switch them out."

"How?"

"I'll meet you in the parking lot or wherever, we'll trade really quickly, it'll be easy. I'll drop mine on the ground, you pick it up for me, no one will even notice." I looked down at the box of chocolates. If we succeeded, no one would be able to tell the difference. "Now go. If anyone's watching you, they're gonna wonder why you're hanging out in this parking lot." I thought of the guard with the ice-blue eyes and wondered if he was still tailing me. The prophet had implied that the guard was no longer following me, but I imagined that might change while I was doing a mission specifically for him. I looked around. It was just me and Jude in here, and I saw no security cameras. It seemed like I was safe so far.

"Okay. Thank you." Jude had put me at ease. We had a plan. We could do this.

"I'll see you in a few," Jude said, flipping his visor down. He drove off, and my stomach reknotted with anxiety.

I drove slowly, wanting to give Jude plenty of time to find the chocolates and meet me at the address. I made a few intentional wrong turns, hoping to seem to anyone monitoring me that I'd simply gotten lost. I circled the block before finally pulling into a parking lot. The parking lot of an elementary school. I was glad I'd taken the pill to ease my guilt, because the thought of bringing these chocolates into a building full of children made me want to scream. I walked very slowly toward the doors, following the instructions I'd received with the package. Jude should be here by now . . . where was he? This parking lot was huge. He could be anywhere. Did he see me?

"Are you here with the package?"

I turned. Squinted at the woman walking toward me, her neat blue dress swishing rhythmically as she walked.

"I . . . I don't . . ." I stammered, trying to buy time.

"A little bird told me a pious young woman was stopping by with a package from the prophet himself. We've all been so excited . . ." Behind the bright bubbly woman, I saw a motorcycle pulling up. Jude held a package that looked just like mine.

I tried to stall longer. "It'll be here in just a minute."

"Is that it?" She looked at the bag I was holding. "What's in there?"

"Chocolates."

"From the prophet?"

"Yeah," I said, knowing I couldn't lie.

The woman laughed. "Look at you, trying to pull my leg."

She tried to take the package from me, but I held tight. "I'm supposed to deliver it to someone directly. A Rebecca Ridgeway?"

The woman waved toward the building, where I saw a pretty young elementary school teacher standing with her class. "Becky!" she called out to the woman. "Your package!"

The second woman walked toward us, and I thought about bolting, thought about warning them of the danger they were about to bite into, but I couldn't. Or I should say, I didn't. I just stood there as the two women took the package from my hands and tore it open.

"Chocolates! He sent you chocolates. You got chocolates from the prophet!" the first woman squealed. Rebecca was practically jumping for joy, ripping through the cellophane.

I took a step away, and then another, faster and faster. I'd done it. They were examining the selection, taking a bite, then another, and I couldn't watch. I couldn't be there when it happened. I walked right past Jude, to my car, and I drove away.

# CHAPTER 3

I should have grabbed it away," I sobbed to Jude days later. "I should have told them, I should have done something, I shouldn't have just run away . . ." He sat next to me on my bed as I ranted on. "I'm a coward."

"You're not a coward. You were trying to do something good. And we don't even know if anything happened."

I'd been watching the news obsessively, certain that "Elementary School Teachers Punished in Parking Lot" would have been a top story, but so far no hits. I'd taken a pill every day since Saturday, but I still felt guilty. "I just have to know," I said.

"You have her name. Here." He held up his phone, where he'd Googled her. No news articles, but the white pages site did list her home address. "Let's go check in on her."

So we drove to Ms. Ridgeway's house, and we sat outside, waiting. We spent hours in that car, watching her neighbors walking their dogs down this quiet, middle-income block. And then, finally, a car pulled into her driveway. A woman got out. "That's her!" I cried.

"She's alive," Jude marveled.

I looked through a pair of binoculars I'd borrowed from my dad. She looked pious as ever—more beautiful, even. "She's fine," I said, not quite sure I believed it.

"So maybe the chocolates were just chocolates."

"Maybe . . ."

Maybe I'd gotten lucky. Maybe this was it, maybe it would all be this easy.

My cell phone rang. It was that number that had been on the business card. "Don't pick it up yet," Jude said.

We drove away, and the number kept calling. "I have to," I said, and finally, I did. "Hello?"

"Thank you for your service, Grace," a voice on the other line said. I didn't recognize it.

"Who is this?" I asked.

"Another friend of the prophet. He's asked me to deliver something to you. Are you home?"

"On my way!" I said brightly.

I dropped Jude off and headed for my house, trembling. A man was waiting on my front porch. One I recognized. A man with ice-blue eyes.

"Good to see you again, Grace."

"You, too," I said weakly.

"The prophet asked me to give you this." The guard handed me a flash drive.

"What is it?"

"A series of simple tasks, things you can do at your own pace. If you feel so moved."

"I live to do the work of Great Spirit!" I said, hoping I was convincing.

The guard smiled, and left. I stared at the flash drive in my hand. I hoped that somewhere on it was my ticket to freedom.

A few hours later, Jude snuck in my bedroom window, and we went through the drive together. It held five folders, each labeled with a person's name. "Do you recognize any of these people?" Jude didn't. Each folder contained a bio, some maps, and a file labeled "Mission."

"Mission! Dun dun dunnnnn. Grace Luther, superspy," Jude teased.

"Stop it," I said, but I still felt a thrill. As much as I feared what was on this drive, I was curious. The world was still full of secrets to unravel.

The first folder we opened was for Nicole Tao, a pious-looking aerobics instructor who worked thirty minutes away. The mission file said to deliver her a vase of flowers, which I could get by contacting the prophet's office. "Is there a way to drug those?" I worried. "Some kind of airborne poison maybe?"

"Who knows. Maybe the prophet just has crushes on these women," Jude quipped.

"Like he had a crush on the Ramseys, I bet." Remembering the way they lay on the ground, dying, gave me pause. I'd been lucky once . . . I didn't want to assume I would be again. I didn't want to be responsible for any more deaths, directly or indirectly.

We moved on through the others. Nothing looked helpful, until at "Dr. David Marko" Jude took control of the mouse.

"Do you know him?"

"No. But I know his lab. Smith-Marko Pharmaceuticals—it's a little research company not far from here. That scientist I told you about, Alexandra Smith—she's been working with us. She's in hiding," Jude explained. "We rescued her from being taken to this prison-lab . . ."

"Prison-lab?"

"Like a work camp for scientists. We've never been inside, but we've heard the stories. All these scientists who have gotten too close to the truth, to discovering what's really happening, they just disappear. Forever. Supposedly they end up at this work camp, doing who knows what kind of experiments, for Prophet Joshua we assume. Their families are threatened, so they'll develop technology for whoever's perpetrating this conspiracy. Alexandra just got grabbed in the middle of the night—some guys shoved her into a van. Dawn intercepted her, saved her. If she was valuable, maybe information about her partner would be, too."

We called Dawn, and I could hear the elation in her voice. "Dr. Smith is the one who found the link between brain chemistry and changes in appearance—she's the reason we've been able to save so many people already. But Dr. Smith lost all the data from her experiments when she lost access to her lab. If we get that data back, we could find out even more, maybe even how to stop all this."

"How would we get it back?" I asked.

Jude pointed to Marko's mission file. "The prophet gave you the entrance codes to the lab."

I skimmed over the file. "He wants me to steal Marko's data, not hers."

"Steal them both. Make copies of them both, and just give the prophet what he wants." Dawn was breathless. "This could be the breakthrough we've been waiting for."

I put us on mute and looked at Jude. "And if I do that, that's enough? You'll feel like you paid your debt?"

Jude considered it. "I think so."

"You'd come with me to Nova Scotia?"

Jude laughed. "That's really where we're going, huh? Nova Scotia?"

I smiled. "So you are coming."

"I'd go anywhere with you." He kissed me—a kiss of hope. For once I was excited about the future, and I tried to push aside the obvious—that I was officially picking a side in this cosmic war, and I had no proof that it was the right one.

# CHAPTER 4

So the plan was in motion. I kissed Jude goodbye, and then kissed him goodbye again. It was hard to get out the door, now that I knew he loved me. But I'd be back soon, with that "breakthrough" data in hand.

The streetlights whizzed by as I drove back into town, to the address marked on the map. Smith-Marko Pharmaceuticals. I parked in the empty lot and stared at the building—lush landscaping, big glass doors, modern interior. I wondered whether this could possibly be another test from the prophet—breaking and entering should make me feel guilty, right? But I reminded myself, not if I was doing it in Great Spirit's name. I shuddered to think of all the things someone could justify doing in the name of Great Spirit. It echoed mankind's warlike past in a way that frightened me. I steadied myself. Old Grace would have been just fine in my shoes. She would get through this mission un-Punished, and so would I.

I tapped the numbers into the keypad, and the door slid open.

I stepped inside—the place was empty, eerie. Lights came on as I walked, following me through the building. Joshua had provided me with a basic floor plan, which led me through winding corridors directly to Dr. Marko's office. It was messy, family photos and scribbled children's drawings mixed in with scholarly articles. I wasn't sure exactly what I was looking for, but I figured copying the contents of Marko's hard drive would suffice.

While the drive was copying, I went on my secondary mission—the missing research of Dr. Alexandra Smith, the files that would let me run away with Jude. A quick search of office nameplates showed that Alexandra's office had been repurposed some time ago. Where would they be keeping her data?

Dawn had told me what to look for, though I struggled to keep the information in my brain. Even then, when the details of Dr. Smith's research were immensely important to me, my eyes had still glazed over when she explained it. I knew I was looking for keywords, big long chemical names.

After a quick rummage through a few other offices, I found a storage closet full of musty filing cabinets. I pulled out a few drawers, then found it, the mother lode—a whole drawer labeled "A. Smith." Copies of her old files that the prophet's operatives hadn't managed to find and destroy. All those matching keywords—my ticket to a lifetime on the run with Jude. I grabbed as many files as I could carry and headed back out into the hallway, where I heard a noise.

I quickly stepped back into the storage room, waiting, listening. The noise was getting closer. Footsteps. And then—a bright light in my eyes. A flashlight. "Who are you?" the voice asked.

# CHAPTER 5

I held my hand up to my eyes, and the light lowered, giving me a view of the man who'd caught me—fortyish, with kind eyes and messy hair. "I'm Amy Thurlow's niece," I said quickly, remembering a name I'd seen on another door earlier. "She sent me to grab some files. She wasn't feeling well and I offered to go get them so she could work at home tomorrow."

The man squinted at me. "Thurlow's niece? Sister's kid or brother's?"

"Sister's," I said, hoping that was the right answer.

The man chuckled a little. "You must have some stories, then."

"Yeah, I've got a few," I joked back, grateful to this faceless woman who was helping my cover.

"Tell me what you're looking for, maybe I can help." He seemed so earnest.

"Oh, I found it all in here," I said, gesturing to the filing cabinets, not knowing how to bluff my way through actual science with an expert.

The man looked at the files in my hands skeptically. "In here?"

"Yep!" I smiled, hoping he'd just go away.

"What's she working on?"

"Oh, I don't know. She started explaining, but I don't remember . . . I'm not so great at science."

He chuckled, going into fatherly mode. "Everyone great at science had to work hard to get there. What if Einstein had been so fatalist? If science is in Amy's blood, it's in yours."

"Maybe it skipped a generation." Before he could attempt to inspire me any further, I said, "Well, she's waiting. Gotta go!"

"Do you need me to walk you out to your car?"

"Nope, I'm okay," I said.

I walked past him, out the door, but he followed behind me, full of concern. "Are you sure?"

"I'm okay!" I repeated.

I kept praying for him to peel off, go somewhere else—and then he did—into Dr. Marko's office. "Have a great night!" he called ahead to me. I realized with dread—I'd been talking to Dr. Marko this whole time.

I slipped out to my car, panicking. The prophet's flash drive was sitting in Marko's computer. Should I go back for it? Would Marko find it? Maybe he wouldn't . . . maybe I could just drive around the block, wait for him to leave, and then sneak back in and grab it. But what if he did find it, with all that incriminating information on it? Then I would be so, so screwed. I had to go back.

So I stepped back into the building, went directly to Marko's office, where he was sitting down at his computer. The drive was untouched. "Hey," I said, trying to draw his attention.

He looked at me. "Well, aren't you the speedy traveler."

"I think my aunt was looking for one more thing. But I can't remember what it was. It was something to do with like a brain chemical. I think the name started with like an 'E' or an 'O' . . ." I sounded like a complete moron.

"Oxytocin?" Dr. Marko asked.

I pretended to be thinking. "Maybe. Something like that but I don't think it was exactly that." I was moving ever so carefully toward his desk, hoping I could reach out and grab the drive without catching his attention.

Marko smiled. "We'll work it out together." I was starting to regret this plan—now the hopelessly helpful Marko was determined to help me solve a problem that had no answer.

"I don't know. There are a lot of chemicals in the world," I said. Marko's unbroken eye contact unnerved me. As close as I was getting, there was no way I could grab the drive without Marko noticing. I looked around desperately for another solution.

My eyes landed on Marko's bookshelf—lots of books on neurochemistry. I grabbed one more or less at random. "I think maybe it's in here? This title seems familiar. Does my aunt have any research related to this?"

I handed him the book, hoping it would distract him for just a moment. "I can't think of anything," he said as he flipped through.

I watched his eyes, flitting across the pages—could he see the computer out of the corner of his eye? I reached out my hand tentatively. Did he notice the movement? Did he notice how nervous I was, could he hear my heart beating wildly? He was still engrossed . . . I had to make my move. I took a deep breath . . . and darted out my hand. Grabbed the drive as quickly as I could. As I put it in my pocket, Dr. Marko looked up, eyed me. Had he seen? "I know what it is," he said.

My adrenaline rushed. "What?"

"Sucrose."

"What's that?"

"Sugar. Just sugar. If she's looking through Dr. Smith's research, I bet that's what she's working on."

He hadn't seen me grab the flash drive . . . but he knew something about Dr. Smith's research. My curiosity got the better of me. "Why sugar?"

"Well, do you have a basic understanding of how the digestive system works? How the food we eat turns into energy?" I didn't really, so he explained, with as much detail and concern as if I were a biology student preparing for a test. I managed to more or less grasp the basics, but it was what he said next that really surprised me. "Every calorie we consume gives our bodies a certain amount of energy. But we're finding, some of that energy is going missing in ways that can't be accounted for."

"What do you mean?"

"Let me give you an example. It's a silly example, but I think it will help. The other day, my wife baked five dozen cookies for my son's class. She put them in a Tupperware container on the counter, and the next morning, she saw there were only four dozen cookies in there. They didn't just disappear—energy can't just disappear, cookies don't just disappear. Someone ate those cookies, but she doesn't know who or when. Could have been one of my sons, could have been me."

"Was it you?" I asked.

"Not the whole dozen," he said, chuckling. "So what we know is, there's energy, sucrose, missing. Energy that has to go somewhere. Dr. Smith was trying to figure out where it was ending up." I saw a look of sadness cross his face, and I realized for all he knew, Dr. Smith had just disappeared one day. The lab was named after both of them—they must have been close.

"What do you think?" I asked him. "Where do you think the energy is going?"

"I'm actually devising an experiment to study just that," he said. "But here I am, talking your ear off. I'm sure Amy's wondering what's taking you so long."

I nodded, a little disappointed that the science lesson was over. "Nice to meet you. Thanks for the help. Sorry to bother you."

"Never a bother. Stop by anytime. Tell Amy I think her niece is a delight."

I blushed, and wondered—as nice as Marko had been, was he still suspicious of me? And if so, did it matter? As long as I got out of here with all the data, I'd be fine. Joshua didn't expect me to be some kind of master spy. Past Marko's inquisitive gaze, I hurried to my car, drive in hand.

I drove back to Jude, handed him the hard copy files, and

made him a copy of everything on the flash drive—Marko's files, as well as the people the prophet seemed to be targeting. "You did a good thing tonight," Jude said.

I smiled, proud. "A breakthrough!"

Jude kissed me, and I was certain I'd never get tired of doing that. I was relieved, and I felt safe for the first time in a very long time. I was going to be able to run away with Jude. Everything was going to be okay. I spent the next couple days dreaming and secretly packing, interrupted only by the doorbell—the guard with ice-blue eyes, coming to take Dr. Marko's data. As I handed over the drive, a chill went down my spine. I tried to push those feelings aside. It would all be worth it.

But something was nagging at me—something didn't feel right. I told myself, *You felt this way last time, and it turned out to be nothing.* I let a day go by, but the feeling didn't pass. And then I saw the news article: "Prominent Neuroscientist, Dr. David Marko, Missing."

It had to be a mistake. I drove in a daze to Smith-Marko again, forgetting any concern for my cover, and I ran inside, past a few confused office workers.

I stood outside his office and looked in—everything was gone. Stripped bare, leaving only strewn family photos. I looked down at those pictures of Marko with his kids . . .

The receptionist had caught up with me, was on edge. "Can I help you?"

"What happened to Dr. Marko?" I asked, knowing the answer.

She seemed a little nervous. "Are you with those people who came here earlier?"

I shook my head, going for a spin on a familiar lie. "I'm his niece. I heard he was missing. I didn't believe it."

She looked at me with sympathy. "You should talk to your family," she said gently. I saw the answer in her eyes. There was no question—Marko had been disappeared just like his colleague. But this time, I was the one responsible.

# CHAPTER 6

Marko's children would grow up without their father. That nice, overly helpful man would be a prisoner. It hit me in the gut. Every moment I'd felt alone since all this madness had started, all the reasons I'd wanted to run away with Jude—I'd just subjected someone else to that same hell, to that same loneliness. To worse, because he was in prison, locked up away from everything and everyone he'd ever loved. I'd been monumentally selfish, trading another person's life for my own. There had to be some way to take it back.

I showed up at Jude's door in a frenzied state. Before I could utter a word, Jude noticed my distress. "What's wrong?"

"Dr. Marko's gone. You have to tell Dawn, maybe she can intercept him . . ."

But then I saw the look on Jude's face. A twinge—he felt guilty. "I'm so sorry, Grace."

"What?"

He tried to figure out how to tell me. "Dawn already knows about Marko."

I was initially relieved. "So she's going to save him?"

He was mumbling, bits of the story squeezing out in dribs and drabs. "Well, sort of. She just told me, I didn't know before . . ."

"What?" I wanted to pull the information out of him.

He took a deep breath. "It wasn't just the data she wanted." I could guess before Jude even said it. "All she needed was his name. She had someone put a tracking device on him. She wanted to find out where they were taking him."

"You mean this whole thing was a setup? She wanted Marko to never see his family again . . ."

"That's not . . ."

"She lied to me!"

Jude tried to calm me down. "Now we know where all the scientists are disappearing to. Look." He pulled up a map on his phone, a dot marking a road in the mountains of West Virginia. "Now we can go in and save everyone else. It's all for a good reason, I promise."

"Why should I believe that? Why wouldn't Dawn just lie again? Placate me, keep me quiet . . ."

"Because I told Dawn I'd help her rescue them. All of them, including Dr. Marko. It's happening tomorrow."

"If that's true, then let me help."

"It's dangerous," he said.

"I don't care about that."

"You should. If I get caught, if any of the others get caught—

we're all people with no identities. People the world thinks are dead. We have no cover to protect, nothing at stake . . ."

"You think you have nothing at stake?" I asked, my anger at him for disappearing coming roaring back.

"*You* have no training . . ."

"I faced down Samuel and Joshua and convinced them I knew nothing. I stole data right out from under Dr. Marko's nose and he never noticed. Tell me again why I'm a liability?"

"Do you know how to shoot a gun? Can you defend yourself if you're attacked?"

"If your plan is to shoot your way in and shoot your way out, you need a better strategy."

"You have a cover to protect. You're valuable."

"Yeah, well my 'cover' got an innocent man wrongly imprisoned. That doesn't seem that valuable to me."

"Dawn will save him."

"She just lied to you! Why do you trust her?"

"She saved my life." I had to admit, I admired his loyalty. "Even if you don't trust her, do you trust me?"

Did I? Should I? If there was any person in the world I should still trust, it was Jude. But there had been so many things I'd trusted that had turned out to be lies. "I trust you," I said, hoping that by saying it, I could make it true.

"Then stay here. And try not to worry about it. If it hadn't been you stealing Dr. Marko's files, it would have been someone else. I don't mean to be callous, but . . . so many terrible things have happened to so many people . . . you can't let yourself feel responsible for every one of them."

"But I *am* responsible for this one. Dr. Marko is a good man.

If I'm willing to put someone away for life like that, I should be willing to be the one to give my life."

It was clear this was not the attitude Jude was expecting. "There's no convincing you of anything, is there?"

"Not anymore," I said, a little proud.

Jude shook his head. "You're a good person, I'll give you that." My heart soared. For the first time since all of this had started, I finally did feel like a good person. And it was that feeling, as much as anything, that made me certain I had to follow through. But Jude's tone was resolute. "I wish you could come. I really do."

"So that's it. You're just taking Dawn's side."

Jude was boiling over with frustration. "Don't throw a tantrum, it's not going to get you anywhere."

I furiously went silent. There was no greater authority I could protest to, no way of winning this fight. And after the way she'd just lied to me, there was no way I trusted Dawn to save Dr. Marko, unless I was there to witness it.

A feeling overtook me, a feeling that I was being compelled to action. It was the first time I'd feel that way, but not the last. I knew in my gut, with a deep kind of certainty, that I couldn't trust Dawn to save Dr. Marko. I had no idea why, or what I was about to do, but I knew I'd have to break into that compound myself.

I pasted on a smile for Jude. "Fine."

And as he stepped away to make some dinner, he left his phone behind. Quickly, before he could see, I snapped a picture with mine—a picture of the location where Dr. Marko was being held. One way or another, I was going to right my wrongs.

# CHAPTER 7

With the GPS on my father's car still disabled, I set out early. I told my dad I was going to a prayer rally with Macy, a lie I knew he'd believe since she'd been attending them any chance she could. As I sped across the West Virginia border, my nerves began to creep up on me. Jude was right—I was risking a lot. Logically I knew this was a terrible idea.

I imagined how angry Jude would be when he found out. Maybe I'd never get to see how angry. Maybe I'd be locked in one of those prison cells like Dr. Marko, or worse. But either way, I knew I was likely giving up my chance to run away with Jude by taking this action. I was on my own now, and it felt right, it felt honest, it felt moral. Though my faith in Great Spirit had been shaken by discovering the truth about the Revelations, this feeling, this certainty that there was something I needed to do, was giving me something to believe in again. Great Spirit had finally put me on the right path, and I was going to follow it through to the bitter end, wherever it took me.

I'd never navigated without a GPS before, and I got lost more than once trying to follow the paper maps I'd bought at a gas station. And then, in my rearview mirror, I saw it—a motorcycle, its driver wearing a blue helmet. Jude. I tried to drive faster to evade him, but he still gained on me, pulled up next to me. Honked.

I pulled over, and the bike screeched to a stop in front of my car. Jude pulled off his helmet as I hopped out. "What are you doing?" he yelled at me.

"Saving Dr. Marko. Why are you following me?"

"To stop you from doing something insanely stupid."

"So I'm insane now. Stupid *and* insane."

"Grace, you don't have any idea what you're walking into, what this place is. You have no plan for how to get in or out. No idea where Marko is, what kind of security he's under . . ."

"I get it!" I said, and I did. "But what else am I supposed to do?"

"Trust me."

"Why should I? You don't trust *me*. You've been following me."

"And if I hadn't been? Do you wish you'd gone into Walden Manor on your own? Do you wish you'd died in your driveway?"

I looked down, a little ashamed.

"You know, Dawn did tell me to keep watching you. That wasn't a lie, I wasn't just trying to push you away. I told her you didn't need to be watched, that you were all right on your own—I told her I trusted you, that you wouldn't do anything that would endanger us . . ."

"And now you're glad you had to babysit me," I spat back.

"If you go in there ahead of us, you blow the whole rescue

operation *and* your cover. You lose any chance of *actually* rescuing Marko. And accomplish what?"

"So what do you want me to do?" I asked. "Wait at home and see if Dawn's being honest this time?"

"Yes!"

"Well, tough," I said, moving back toward the car.

Jude sighed. "Fine. You wanna come? We'll give you a front-row seat." Jude pulled something from his bag—an ugly wig with long thick hair. I took it.

"This is for me?"

"If you're going to risk your life anyway, you might as well try to help."

"I thought I was too valuable to help."

"Well . . . there's no convincing you of anything anymore, is there?" Jude gave me a little smile, an olive-branch smile.

I took the wig, wrapping my arms around him. "Thank you."

"Don't die, okay?"

"Same to you," I said.

Jude grinned. "I died once. I wasn't a fan."

So I'd forced my way onto the mission . . . hopefully that would be enough to satisfy the voice that nagged me in my head. Though I knew Jude was right, that every argument he made was completely logical, I couldn't shake this feeling in the pit of my stomach. There was still something wrong with this plan, I still shouldn't be trusting Dawn to mount this operation. But I pushed those feelings aside, dismissed them as paranoia. I'd been wrong so often recently, of course I'd be distrustful, of course I'd want to handle everything myself. But Jude . . . I knew Jude, I'd known him for so long. He was smart, he had the kindest heart I'd known, and he'd been dealing with these people for far longer than I had. If Jude believed this was the best way to save Marko, I had to trust him.

A half hour or so later, an eighteen-wheeler rolled up next to us, driven by a big guy with a red beard who Jude told me was named Owen—another rescued man with no traceable identity. Owen glared at me as he opened the back of the truck, clearly not pleased I'd shoehorned my way into this expedition. "Get in." Owen scowled. Jude gave me an apologetic look and a pill—the nasty kind, to disguise my face—before getting into the passenger seat. I hid deep in the cargo container behind cartons of fruits and vegetables, and the truck rumbled ahead.

After an hour or more of lurching back and forth up winding mountain roads, the truck finally stopped. "Produce delivery," I could faintly hear Owen say.

A second muffled voice, "Can I see your badges?" Then, "I'm just going to take a look in the back."

I closed my eyes and held my breath as sunlight streamed in. I could hear cartons near me scraping against the metal walls. The guards were searching the truck. Methodically, working their way back to where I was hidden.

The door slammed shut. Darkness again. "Have a nice day," the voice said, and the truck lumbered forward.

We were in.

# CHAPTER 8

Owen drove the truck across a dirt road, where we bumped along for a mile or so. Once we were well inside, Owen opened up the back and let me ride in the front, so it'd seem like I was part of their team when we approached the prison. The compound was massive and strangely beautiful, full of trees. I couldn't help but marvel at the landscape as we drove.

On the side of the road, I saw a little shack with a guard sitting out front, rifle in hand. He watched the truck as we rolled by. I realized I was staring at him, wondered if my expression conveyed the fear that was trembling through me. I quickly averted my eyes and tried to appear nonchalant as we rumbled past.

We arrived at another rustic-looking building. The architecture, mixed with the idyllic scenery, gave off a strange summer-camp vibe. Owen hopped out, calling out to Jude, "Unload the truck." He still wouldn't make eye contact with me.

Owen headed off, and Jude told me he was going to disable

the security systems, so we could gain access to the cells. That left Jude and me to corral the scientists and get them to the meeting point without being discovered. Easier said than done. As we started unloading the boxes of produce that were our cover, I felt a rush of adrenaline. There was no turning back now.

I took a deep breath as we stepped into the homey lobby of the building—hardly a high-tech-lab setting, from the looks of it. More like a kitschy, woodsy retreat. Plaid couches in the waiting room, a fireplace in the corner. Security cameras blinked ominously on every wall. We passed a woman in a stiff black uniform. "Kitchen?" Jude asked her.

"Down the hall to your left," she said with a warm smile. When she glanced at me though, her expression darkened. It seemed the employees here still believed that beauty and goodness were one and the same. My near-Outcast disguise might have gotten me inside, but it wouldn't win me anyone's trust now that I was here.

As we made our way toward the kitchen, I struggled under the weight of the box I was carrying but tried not to show it. This was my "profession" after all—I had to look the part. I handed off the produce with a smile to the other kitchen workers, who gave me similarly disgusted looks. But after a couple dozen trips, sweating an embarrassing amount, I couldn't help looking tired. Jude noticed. "It's almost time," he said, eyeing the clock on the wall. I looked around at all the workers milling about. I couldn't understand how we were ever going to sneak away.

And then—"Troops! Morning meeting." I watched as everyone but Jude and me gathered around a woman in a trim black suit.

"Let's go," Jude whispered, pulling me by the arm out into the hallway. Where we were finally alone.

He tossed something at me—a stiff black uniform, like the other workers had been wearing. I hastily threw it on over my other clothes, as Jude did the same. The thick material hung off of me, clearly made for someone twice my size. I looked ridiculous. But Jude was already heading down the hall, so I hiked up my pants, pushed up my sleeves, and jogged after him.

I tried not to look at the security cameras eyeing us from every wall as we rounded corner after corner. Jude had this place memorized, and I followed blindly behind him. Finally, we reached a big, heavy metal door. It seemed different from the rest of this place—more secure. There were secrets hidden behind it, I could tell just by looking at it.

Jude quickly entered a number on the keypad next to it, then pulled on the handle with all his weight . . .

And standing on the other side was a guard, wearing a uniform like ours. He eyed us, putting a hand on the gun at his hip. "Are you new?"

"Yeah, we're training," Jude said.

"Can I see your badges?" the guard asked.

"I've got them right here," Jude said, reaching into his pocket. And then, lightning fast, Jude punched the guy in the jaw, and he collapsed to the floor. I stifled a scream, as Jude stoically hopped over the guard. I looked down—the guy was unconscious. "Grace!" Jude hissed, and I ran after him.

# CHAPTER 9

I felt nauseous. Who was this version of the boy I loved, who could take out an armed guard with a single punch? I knew he'd become tougher since he'd disappeared, but I hadn't imagined him as a fighter.

"He's not dead," Jude reassured me, reading the horror in my expression. I nodded, though I didn't want to imagine how injured that guard would be when he woke up. I'd wanted to ally myself to the most moral side in this conflict. If this was what Jude had become after two years, how would fighting for Dawn transform me?

Jude pulled me down a stairwell, into the high-ceilinged, dank basement of the building. We walked across a catwalk overlooking rows and rows of cells that were more like cages—bars on every side. Thousands of people were crammed in here together. Their voices buzzed below us in a low, miserable hum. "Follow me," Jude said.

We found a bank of switches, thousands of them, all along

a wall, all numbered. "These unlock the cells," Jude whispered. "We just have to wait for Owen to take out the security system."

I nodded, shaking, nervous. "What happens if he can't do it?" Jude's silence made me think he was worried about that, too.

I looked down at the rows of cells and saw a few people dressed in black strolling between them. Guards. I pointed them out. "Is that a problem? Those guards?"

"When the security goes down, we'll create a diversion."

But as the minutes wore on, I began to get nervous. It seemed like something wasn't going according to plan. I could tell Jude was unsettled, too. I tried to think, tried to come up with some alternative. "I could create the diversion now," I suggested. "And you could get the others . . ."

Jude shook his head, interrupting. "The moment we open the doors to the outside, we'll trip an alarm. There's no way you can distract every guard on the whole compound."

"There's gotta be some other way."

Jude considered. And as he was considering, the lights went out.

"What happened?" I whispered.

"Someone cut the power," he whispered back. Not the plan, I could tell from his voice.

"Was it Owen?" I asked.

"If it wasn't, we're screwed anyway." He handed me a flashlight. "Hold this for me." I did. He pulled out a piece of paper with a bunch of numbers written on it and methodically started flipping the switches that matched those numbers. After a moment, he double-checked his work. Then he moved to another section of the wall and flipped ten more switches, all numbers preceded by "C." He pointed to the ten. "These guys are all on that block on the right. C Block. Send them out that far right door. We're not trying to rescue them; they're the diversion. They'll run right past the guard station, and the guards will spend their time trying to catch them, while we sneak out the back." I nodded.

We watched as the guards moved—it was like a chess game, waiting for them to disappear into just the right row, one with no prisoners we needed to rescue. Jude watched, waited. Then— "Go, go now."

I tiptoed down the catwalk stairs, trying to avoid making any sounds. Eerie green emergency lighting glowed in the aisles between the cells, and I could see half-silhouetted faces peeking out at me from behind the bars.

A big guy leered in my direction. "Hey. You. Wanna come pray with me? Bet you've got a pretty face under there." These people, the ones still locked in the cells—they must not be scientists, I realized, since Jude hadn't freed them. I wondered what they were doing here, why we weren't rescuing them. I ducked my head, away from their curious looks and prodding insults.

I got to C Block. "Hey, lady, I think I need a little discipline," an older man jeered at me. I looked at the number above his cell—it was one of the ones Jude had unlocked. Great. I pulled the door open then stepped back, nervous about what this guy might do as a freed man.

"I'm here to rescue you," I told him quietly. "Run out the

doors to your right. Down the corridor, you'll get to the other end of the building. You don't have much time—go now." The guy took another look at me. I wondered if he sensed the lie, the trap I was leading him into. He took a step forward, as I took another back. And then he hurried off down the corridor I'd directed him to.

I freed another man, then another. As the prisoners' footsteps echoed softer and softer, I heard another set of footsteps approaching. A guard, heading my direction.

He hadn't seen me yet. I quickly stepped into an open cell and closed the door, watching the guard roam up and down my aisle, peering in at all of us. I turned my head, trying to disappear into the shadows, hoping the guard wouldn't recognize that I wasn't one of his prisoners, that I was wearing the same black uniform he was. "We've got nine missing down here," the guard called out. More guards swarmed into the row, and I stared steadfastly at the floor.

"Who let them out?"

"Must be part of the power failure."

The guard pulled on a set of bars nearby. "These ones are still locked though." The guards pulled on bars all down the row. Approaching mine.

As one guard approached my cell, he paused. Turned away from me. "I'll go reset the locks." He headed toward the catwalk, never checking my cell. I breathed a sigh of relief. I couldn't leave yet, not while there were still guards patrolling my aisle, but I had a moment of respite.

"So what's wrong with me?" the prisoner next to me asked. I dared not make eye contact, dared not encourage him further.

If the guards overheard, they might guess I was the intruder. But he continued, "You like Fredricks and Bogart better than me? You don't wanna rescue me? Come on, answer . . ."

That voice . . . I looked up. And I almost fainted. There in the cell next to me was Ciaran.

# CHAPTER 10

I tried to recover from the shock. And I thought back—had I actually seen Ciaran dead? No, I'd just heard the gunshot, seen him go down from far away, in the dark, and assumed . . . but here he was. Staring right at me. Turns out I hadn't been lying to his parents after all.

Did he recognize me? Not in the wig, not with my face like this. But he knew I was from the outside, knew I'd been part of the rescue party. And knowing him, he had plenty of incentive to blow my cover if he wanted to. I pulled myself together and whispered toughly, "Be quiet, and I'll get you out."

He looked at me—did he recognize my voice? "Why? Who are you?"

"A friend," I said. I watched the guard manning the aisles. Moving away from me. Could I sneak out? Get to Jude on the other side of this massive room? The guard neared the end of the aisle. Turned the corner. The moment the guard was out of sight, I ran for the cell door, but it was locked. I rattled the bars.

I looked up at the catwalk, where I saw a guard standing by the switches Jude had used to unlock the cells. They'd reset everything, locked me in.

"Friend, huh? Looks like we're gonna get to be real friendly," Ciaran said with a smile. "I'd be glad to show you the ropes here."

"How long have you been in here?" I asked. I had so many questions, and I was as terrified of Ciaran's answers as I'd been eager to hear Jude's.

"A couple weeks," Ciaran said.

"Why? What did you do?"

He shrugged. "Who knows. Some stupid shit probably."

*You tried to rape me! You think that's "stupid shit"?* I wanted to scream, but I held my tongue. With a calm voice, I asked, "Is there any other way out?"

"Oh yeah, your cell has a back door, leads to a lovely patio with a hammock." Ciaran snickered.

"What is this place? Do you know who runs it? Who brought you here?"

"You don't know? I thought you were my great savior."

Ugh, this was going nowhere. "I'm just trying to help you. If you don't want to be helped, not my problem," I hissed at him.

Ciaran was up against the bars that separated us—was able to squeeze a finger through. "I'd love your help." He leered.

Seeing him, talking to him—it made me sick. I leaned against the opposite wall, as far as I could get from him. Finally, I heard more footsteps running toward me. Jude.

"Are you okay?" he asked.

"I'm locked in," I said, demonstrating.

Jude pulled out a key ring. "It's on here somewhere."

As Jude went through the keys, Ciaran moved forward. "Another friend?" Ciaran asked.

"We're only gonna get you out if you stay quiet," I said to Ciaran, hushed. And gave Jude a look—don't engage.

Jude found the key, unlocked the door. He whispered, "We've got everybody but one."

"Who's left?" I asked. Jude's look told me the answer. The one person I was here to rescue hadn't been rescued yet.

As we ran off, Ciaran called after us, "Hey!" But I didn't look back. Up on the catwalk, a guard was busy inspecting the switches. If at any moment he looked down and saw us . . .

Jude grabbed my arm, pulled me into an aisle. A different guard ran by, a half second away from catching us.

Once he was out of sight, Jude whispered, "We've got five minutes. See if you can make any headway."

As Jude tossed me the keys, I turned—there was Dr. Marko. Sitting in his open prison cell. "Dr. Marko!" I whispered. He looked up. "I'm here to rescue you. Let's go!" I said.

But he just stared at me. Shook his head. "No, you're not."

"Yes, I am. You have to go."

He looked me dead in the eyes. "You don't know what you're doing."

"I know exactly what I'm doing. I'm not leaving without you. You're going home."

Marko's face filled with sadness. His stare was eerie. "There is no going home."

# CHAPTER 11

We'll find a way to keep you safe, we'll put you into hiding . . ."

"You don't understand."

I could hear footsteps running toward us. Guards? "If he won't come, we have to go," Jude hissed, but I shook my head. I couldn't leave without Dr. Marko.

"What don't I understand?" I asked him.

"I can't leave. None of us can—there's this thing in my head." I looked at Jude. Clearly he'd heard this all already, and he shrugged, not knowing how to help.

The footsteps were getting closer. "What do you mean, something in your head?" I asked.

"If I leave this building, I'll die."

Jude nudged me again, and I saw a guard approaching. I closed Marko's cell door, locked it. "Any others still open?" I called out to the guard.

The guard looked at me, trying to place me. Then shook his head. "I'll check the next aisle."

As the guard moved off, I turned back to Marko. "The people I'm with, they know everything about this place. I think they'd know if there was something in your head."

"There's a perimeter around the compound," Marko said. "This technology, it can sense when we cross it. Cross it and you die, that's what they told us. It happened to a guy before I got here."

"But all the other scientists left," I said. "They've already gone to the meeting point. Why would they do that if leaving would kill them?" I asked.

"They've been here longer than I have," Marko said solemnly. "Their families have been threatened, they've been forced to invent unspeakable things. They want out one way or another." One way or another. Suicide.

Jude seemed as horrified as I was. "Our team must have some way to disable it."

"There's no way," Marko told him.

"They wouldn't have brought us out here if there was no way to get you out," I repeated, hoping it was true. "They wouldn't have launched a useless mission."

"Maybe they didn't know," Marko pointed out. "You didn't know."

"Sometimes they keep things from us," I said, summoning all the goodwill I had toward Dawn. "For our own protection. They tell us what we need to know because otherwise we might make the wrong decisions." I wasn't sure if any of it was true or not, but

I couldn't leave Marko here. I had to at least get him to the meeting point with the others, see if there was a way to get him out.

"I don't know . . ."

"Please, come with me," I begged him. "If there's any chance I can get you out alive . . ."

"You can't."

"Just to the meeting point outside. If they can't deactivate the thing in your head, we'll put you right back in here," I said. "You've got nothing to lose."

Marko looked at Jude, then back to me. "Just to the meeting point."

Relieved, I unlocked his cell, and he jogged with us down the halls. We ran out the back doors, deep into the woods, to the spot where we'd agreed to reconvene with Owen. A couple dozen scientists were already loading themselves into the back of the truck, into the cartons that had once held produce. They'd be perfectly hidden.

We ran up to Owen, who was looking over a set of paper maps. "We have a problem," Jude said.

I looked to Marko, waiting for him to explain, but Owen interrupted. "The transmitters, right?"

I wished I was as surprised as Jude was by Owen's casual admission of dishonesty. Jude explained, through clenched teeth, "He said there was something in his head, yeah."

Owen turned to Marko. "When I cut the power, I disabled the perimeter. When we cross the line, the transmitter in your head won't know. It'll be safe to get you out of here for another fifteen minutes."

Marko looked relieved, but Jude was furious. "You knew about this before we got here?"

Owen was unfazed. "We didn't know if the plan would work. We didn't want to alarm anyone."

"But you couldn't tell me? Vital information . . ."

"What can I say, Dawn's orders."

"You are unbelievable," Jude shot back, as Owen moved off to help the last few scientists into the truck.

I hung back, letting Jude process his anger. "Are you okay?" I asked.

"What if something had gone wrong? What if we'd gotten separated? I could have taken someone across too early . . ." He didn't seem to want to think about that possibility. "It's ridiculous. I'm here, I'm trying to help, I've done everything I can for these people . . ."

"I'm sorry," I said, hugging him.

His voice got softer. "You were right. You knew we couldn't trust them."

"But I still shouldn't have tried to rescue Dr. Marko on my own with no information," I admitted.

"I'm glad you did. Because it's what got you here, and we wouldn't have gotten Marko out of that cell without you convincing him."

I looked over at Owen, who was helping Marko into the back of the truck—time for us to go, too. As we walked back, I asked Jude, "Are they really the good guys?"

"They saved my life. They're not the bad guys," Jude insisted.

I hopped into the back of the truck as Jude closed the door behind me. "I'll see you on the other side."

I squeezed into a carton next to a middle-aged female scientist. I could feel the heat from all the squirming, breathing bodies. "Here we go," the woman across from me said as the truck rumbled forward.

The bumps felt bigger this time—the truck was moving faster. We had a deadline to make. Finally we slowed to a stop. I could hear the mumbled voices of the guards outside. "We gotta take a look in the back."

"How come?" Owen's voice asked, annoyed.

"Extra security measure today. Because of the power outage." Because of the prison break.

"Of course," Owen said. I heard the footsteps moving toward the back of the truck. A hand fumbling with a latch. And then—a lurch.

Owen was flooring it. The truck sped away from the gate, and everyone in the back of the truck cried out as we were tossed backward.

Gunshots rang out, lots of them, from behind us. Our screams were deafening inside the container.

The truck turned sharply, going off-road, the ride getting bumpier.

I peeked my head out of the carton, saw that the other scientists were doing the same. A bullet shot through the container above our heads. Everyone ducked, hugged the floor in fear.

I saw Dr. Marko nearby, eyes closed, counting. Calculating how far we'd driven, I suspected. How far until we reached the "perimeter."

The woman next to me was praying. "God, please . . . I'll do whatever You want me to do; I'll go back there . . ." I took her hand, started to pray with her. She smiled at me.

And then the ground fell out from underneath us as the scientists and the cartons and I were slammed back and forth. The truck was on deeply uneven terrain, headed down a steep hill off-road.

More screams as bodies slammed into the ceiling.

The truck hit solid ground again, and we all hurtled back toward earth. My limbs were aching, bruised . . .

But the gunshots had ceased. We all remained quiet, listening . . . and we felt the truck stabilize. We were back on a paved road, hurtling down the mountain.

"Is that it?" one of them asked.

"I don't know. Did we already cross the perimeter?"

"Now," Dr. Marko said. Everyone looked at him. "We're crossing it now."

He closed his eyes, bracing himself. The others continued to pray, began to shake, held each other's hands.

"In case this is it," one man said, "it's been lovely being imprisoned with all of you."

But the truck drove on. And the scientists kept looking around at each other, watching, waiting.

"Nothing's happening," a young woman whispered.

"They really did it! They disabled the perimeter!"

"Is that really it?" another asked.

They began cheering and celebrating, hugging each other as best they could, crammed into the back of that truck.

"Do you have a phone?" one of them asked me. "I want to call my wife."

"I don't, I'm sorry," I said.

"What are they going to do with us now?" another wondered.

My stomach filled with dread. "I assume they'll put you into hiding somewhere. So the people from that compound can't find you. Maybe they'll let your families go with you? Or maybe they have some other plan, I don't know," I said, watching the mixed emotions on their faces. I wanted so badly to give them the good news they all wanted to hear. That they were going back to their lives before prison. But I had a feeling that wasn't going to happen, for any of us.

The woman I'd shared a carton with was smiling. "I'll get to meet my grandbabies."

"More than one?" the man next to her asked.

"My daughter was pregnant with twins. Gave birth a few months ago. I haven't even gotten to see a picture."

And then I noticed her nose was dripping blood. The man next to her noticed, too. "Hey, you've got a little . . ." He pointed.

She put her hand to her face, concerned. "What?" And then she collapsed.

The other scientists began to scream, stand, run to her, move away from her. "She's passed out." "Is she okay?" "What happened?" "Why is it just happening to her?" "She's not responding." "Someone get some water, something!"

But it wasn't just her. Many of them were bleeding. They had their hands to their faces, feeling it, realizing what was happening. One by one, they all began to drop.

I started banging on the wall of the truck, trying to get Jude and Owen's attention. "Stop! Help!" I screamed louder, desperate, but the truck kept moving, and the scientists kept wailing, crying, falling.

A body slumped on top of me—Dr. Marko, bleeding like all the rest of them. Dead. I looked around. I was surrounded, smothered, by a pile of dead bodies.

# CHAPTER 12

I screamed and screamed and screamed, but the truck rumbled on, down the hills, throwing me back and forth from one dead body into another. I began to cry, pray, grow delirious. They weren't going to stop, I realized. They either didn't know or didn't care that all their passengers but one were dead.

I tried to imagine them still alive, hoped that the movements of gravity that rocked them around were signs of life. But as the truck jostled us, I felt their blood, their lifeless weight on top of me. Denial gave way to panic, gave way to horror.

After a while I became numb to it; it just became my state of being. *I am a person who lives in the middle of this pile of dead bodies, and that's totally normal. It's a totally normal way to get from one place to another.*

Finally, after twenty minutes that felt like twenty days, the truck stopped, and a sliver of light came through—we'd stopped in a tunnel. A silhouetted figure looked in. "Oh."

Owen hopped into the truck bed, knelt to take the pulses

of the scientists closest to the door. I saw Jude standing outside, horrified. "Grace? Grace!"

"I'm over here." My voice came out as a squeak.

He jumped inside, picked his way through to me. Extended a hand, pulled me up, out of the carnage. "It's okay. I'm here. I've got you."

I grabbed onto him, sobbing. "They're dead, they're all dead." Jude looked around, disbelieving, as I turned on Owen. "You said the perimeter was disabled."

"We thought it was," Owen said, shaken.

"Liar!" I screamed.

"Why would I lie about that? Do you think I'm a monster? Do you think I wanted this to happen?"

"You keep lying, you all keep lying," I sputtered, out of control. Jude put a hand on my back, trying to calm me down, but I wasn't going to calm down. "You give me one good reason why I don't turn you in to the prophet for mass murder."

"Okay, you wanna know the truth?" Owen looked me in the eye, confrontational. "I disabled the perimeter. But we didn't know how these things worked for sure. There's two ways they could have been designed. One way, the thing in their brains gets a signal when they cross the perimeter, that signal is what drops them dead. Shut down the perimeter, you're good, everyone gets out alive. The other way . . . the thing in their brains needs a signal to *keep* them alive. You shut down the perimeter, they stop getting any signal at all . . . and they die, some amount of time later. It's like a kill switch."

"If you weren't sure . . ."

"Dawn told you, I know she did—the technology they were

working on in there? Any day now, they were gonna reach completion. And once that happened, any day they could've dropped it like a bomb on every innocent person in the world. We didn't have time to work out a perfect plan to save every scientist. We had to end that project now, before any more damage could be done."

"You are a monster," I said, still shaking.

"No, I just saved your life, and the lives of everyone you know, so shove it."

I stared at him with rage as a pickup truck pulled up next to us.

"That's our ride," Owen said, jumping out to meet the driver.

Once he was gone, I looked over at Jude. He was despondent, desperate, his voice shaking. "This is all my fault . . ."

"It's Dawn's fault," I told him. "You didn't know."

He shook his head. "But I trusted her. You didn't, and I did. And because I did, I led every single one of these people to their deaths." I squeezed his hand, glad he was still on my side. Though I didn't say it, and the upper pill Jude handed me kept it from showing on my face, I felt the same guilt he did. That feeling in my gut—Great Spirit or whatever it was—had told me something was wrong before we started the mission. I'd been the one to convince Dr. Marko to come. By trying to save him, I'd been the one to kill him.

And then, something miraculous—from the pile of bodies, I saw movement. "Jude!" I cried, pointing. A hand was moving—Dr. Marko's.

"Dr. Marko!" Jude ran to him, supported him up. "He's breathing."

"Dr. Marko, can you hear us?" I asked him.

He opened his eyes—looked around the truck bed, saw the devastation. "Oh . . ."

"You're okay," I said, overjoyed. I hugged him, and he winced.

"Careful, sweetheart." He noticed my face, now returned to its normal, pious state, and his brow furrowed. "It's you."

My shame at being called out as his file thief was overpowered by my relief that he was alive enough to do it. "Yeah. It's me. I thought you were dead."

"Me, too."

"Will the others be okay?" I asked, hopeful.

Marko shook his head. "It doesn't look so promising."

"But you—you're alive," Jude said.

"Maybe because I'm new? The bugs start replicating as soon as you're infected, but I was only there a couple days . . ."

"Bugs?" I interrupted.

"The transmitters," he said. "Nanotech." He must have seen my blank expression, because he quickly explained, "Nano means small, tech means . . . tech. It's a network of tiny little machines. They sit in your brain, feeding on the sugars in your bloodstream, waiting on an input—you know, checking to see if we've passed the perimeter. The guys at that prison camp infected me with them the moment I got here. These ones anyway."

These ones. It all clicked into place. I looked at Jude, I could tell we were thinking the same thing. "There's more than one kind . . ."

"Exactly," Dr. Marko said. "You can make a little computer do just about anything. An input could be neural spiking when you've activated the region of your brain associated with guilt.

That'd be the prefrontal cortex, by the way, where your conscience lives. So this network measures your conscience and
judges you based on it. Output, these machines could affect
your hormones, make you healthy, unhealthy . . ."

"Make your throat close up," Jude said softly.

Marko nodded, solemn. "Yep. Found that out on day one of
lockup. That's the big secret, the reason for all the Punishments.
The Revelations were never Great Spirit—they were orches-
trated by the scientists I was locked up with."

It all began to make sense. "So the tech in our brains—it was
invented by someone working for the prophet?"

"So it seems."

"And we all have these in our blood."

"Tens of thousands of them, each and every one of us. All
you've gotta do is breathe one in, and they'll replicate in your
bloodstream. Invisible to the naked eye. Spray them out over a
city, and suddenly every single person's infected." He looked to
me. "Remember that experiment I wanted to do? I don't have to
do it anymore. I already know who's been eating the cookies." At
Jude's look of confusion, he added, "Long story."

"So the nanotech runs off the sugars in my blood?"

"Genius, isn't it? An endless power source. They'll run until
you die. Once your brain activity ceases, they're designed to
stop working and self-destruct. The waste hides in your cells, so
you can dissect human brains all day and never find them."

"But what you have in your brain, the transmitter, the thing
that almost killed you—that's different?" Jude asked.

"Newer. Deadlier. But same idea. Yours Punish you for feeling guilt, mine give me an aneurysm for leaving prison." He

looked at us. "But both of those are just the beginning. Like I said, you can get a computer to do almost anything."

"What's next?" I asked.

"I was only in the lab a couple days, so I didn't really get the full picture, but . . . your friend, the awful one with the beard—he's not wrong to be afraid. You slowed them down for sure, but . . . Joshua can always abduct other scientists, find other facilities. I'd guess six months from now, they'll be ramping up production on the projects we just abandoned. Truly terrifying days are coming."

I tried to put that thought out of my head. "We're just glad you're okay."

"'Okay' is a strong word. My head hurts like a mother," Dr. Marko said. "Also, not to be demanding, but maybe I should see a doctor or something?"

Jude stepped out of the truck to find Owen, who wasn't nearly as overjoyed at Marko's recovery—he spoke like it was a problem to be dealt with rather than a miracle. We helped Dr. Marko out of the container and into the bed of the pickup truck. We all hid under a blanket in the back of the pickup as we rumbled out of that tunnel, away from the truck full of dead bodies.

When we arrived where I'd met up with Jude and Owen, we loaded Dr. Marko into my dad's car, taking care to lay down blankets to sit on so we wouldn't bloody the seats. Owen thankfully sped out of our lives on Jude's motorcycle.

"Where do we take him?" I asked. "Joshua will know if we take him to a hospital."

"I know where," Jude said, putting a lead foot on the gas pedal.

"How are you doing back there, Dr. Marko?" I asked as we drove through a densely forested back road.

"Okay," he said. I could hear that he was getting sleepy, and I knew that with a potential brain injury, we had to keep him conscious. I intermittently reached back and poked him as we drove, making sure he didn't fall asleep.

"Does my wife know I'm okay?" Dr. Marko asked.

"Not yet," I said. "She'll be so happy to hear." I looked at Jude. Neither of us knew if Marko would ever get to see his family again.

We pulled up to a nondescript house in the far suburbs of D.C. "Where are we?" I asked, but Jude shook his head.

I followed as he moved to the door, knocked. An older man answered, someone I'd never seen before.

"Jude?" The concern in the man's voice made me think this was someone Jude was close to.

Jude gestured to the car, where he could see Dr. Marko had slumped in the backseat. "We need a doctor."

The man looked, nodded. "Bring him inside."

Jude must have noticed the wary way the man was looking at me, because he quickly added, "She's with us. Grace, Father Dennehy . . . Father Dennehy, Grace." I remembered the name—this was the priest who had saved Jude after the car accident, ferried him away to his new life. This was who would be taking in Dr. Marko until Dawn's resistance figured out something else to do with him. The man smiled, shook my hand, and opened the door to welcome us inside.

The house was modest, with a large cross on the wall. While the priest called a doctor he knew we could trust, Jude brought

Marko inside. Jude filled in Father Dennehy on everything—the mission, the lies, the dead scientists. Father Dennehy shook his head, growing more and more concerned as Jude spoke. "Dawn's getting desperate," he told Jude. "She thought we would have accomplished more by now. Desperate people are dangerous."

"Can't you do anything?" Jude asked.

"Dawn thinks she's doing what's right. I can't say I know she's wrong . . . but I know I wouldn't have the stomach for it. For any of it. Priests don't make great generals."

"Why not?" I interjected. "You'd do what's right—that's the best kind of general."

Father Dennehy laughed a little. "I know my limits. Spiritual counsel, that's the path God intended for me. Baptisms, weddings . . ."

"Saving lives," Jude said, smiling his thanks.

"You always have a safe haven here," the priest told Jude.

When the doctor arrived, we watched nervously as she examined Dr. Marko. After twenty minutes or so, she gave us the all clear. "Your friend is going to be just fine."

I was relieved. "We'll see you soon, I hope!" I told Dr. Marko as Jude said his goodbyes to Father Dennehy. I really did hope that.

Jude and I drove home in uncomfortable silence. When we got close to his village, Jude took a deep breath. "What now?" he asked.

"I don't know. I think that's up to you."

He looked at me. "Nova Scotia?"

The dark expression I'd been wearing was finally lit by a smile. "You still want to?" I asked.

"It's about time."

# CHAPTER 13

We made a plan. Tomorrow night, he'd pick me up at the site of the crash, and we'd drive north and meet his friends in Rochester. He said he had a few loose ends to tie up before we left, so I'd have to go to school, make everything look normal before disappearing.

Once I came downstairs from showering off all that blood and grime, my father didn't even ask where I'd been all day. I smiled, played the good daughter—I could do it one last time. We played backgammon. He told me about the sermon he was writing for next Sunday's service, and I gave him some feedback. As he headed to bed, I gave him a hug, a long one. "I love you, Daddy."

"I love you, too." I was glad those would be the last words we ever spoke to each other in person. Once I was in Rochester, I'd call and tell him about the last-minute opening on a volunteer trip to Honduras—I'd give him no time to question my story.

It felt surreal to walk the halls of my school again, to have the same superficial conversations with the same pretty people. Instead of my usual crowd, I was drawn to the kids I never would have deigned to chat with before, the Outcasts I used to look down on. *Do you know the truth?* I wanted to ask them. *What has your life been like, looking the way you do? What do you feel guilty about?* For the first time in my life, I saw their true beauty.

Macy was back in school, and I was glad. I wanted to see her one last time before disappearing forever. She was covered in thick makeup, a funny hat, and she sat at her desk in every class with her head down, her hands blocking her face. She got quite a few stares, some whispers, but overall I was surprised at how nice people were to her. Much nicer than I would have been, had I not known the truth. I realized then what an ugly, petty person had been hidden by my beauty and piety, and I vowed never to be that girl again.

Macy talked excitedly of the future, of the religious camps her parents were sending her to. She would live her life immaculately from now on, she was sure of it. I could see that prayer was slowly restoring her. I had to tell myself that, at least. Otherwise the guilt would have shown on *my* face, for not being able to save her from a less-than-perfect life, from her own ignorance.

At lunch, not wanting to sit in a crowd full of pious automatons, I took my sandwich to a tree a block or so from the school, where I'd seen stringy-haired Ann and some other Outcast kids sit before. I'd come here once with Great Books, proud of my good deeds. Now, as I approached, they immediately vacated— they were tired of hearing my sermons. I wanted to call out and tell them to stay, tell them I understood, that I was on their side now—but what would it matter? I'd be gone in a matter of hours.

As I sat, looking up at the tree, taking in the last warmth I'd feel before disappearing into the Canadian wilderness, someone sat down beside me. It was Dawn. Disgusted to see her, I immediately stood, started walking away, but she followed me, whispered, "You're being watched."

My breath caught in my throat. "Watched?"

"Starting this afternoon. Someone within Prophet Joshua's organization noticed that the GPS on your dad's car is deactivated, and now they're suspicious. My sources tell me they're putting 24/7 surveillance on you."

"I have to go now, then." I told her about my plan with Jude. She didn't seem particularly surprised to hear about it, nor was she particularly supportive.

"You could go," Dawn said. "Maybe you'll get caught, but maybe you'll get across the border and be okay. Or . . . you could stay. You could help us."

I was stupefied that she would even suggest it. "Why in the world do you think I'd say yes to that?"

"Because of this." She handed me an iPad, and I scrolled through the images—the black market, burned to the ground. I swiped quickly past the mangled bodies, horrified.

"Who did this?"

"Who do you think?"

Prophet Joshua. My stomach sank as I remembered telling Samuel about the black market. Its location. Could this be my fault?

"These people deserve justice," she said.

"And you're the one to give it to them?" I asked, incredulous.

"You helped us save countless lives yesterday. I know, those lives are all theoretical, and I can't take away what you had to witness. But you saved so many more. Not to mention all the information Dr. Marko is bringing us . . . we may finally have a shot at understanding this technology for real . . ."

"It's easy to say something's justified when you're the one who did it," I spat back. "You're just finding excuses."

Her voice remained measured. "Maybe I am."

"And you're okay with that? Knowing that there could have been a better path and you didn't take it?"

"You think there was a better path? Tell me, what would you have done?"

"How should I know? You lie to me about everything."

"So say I stop. Say I tell you everything I know, empower you as fully as I can."

"And?"

"Find a way to do it better. If you think there's a more moral road, stay here and help me take it."

"I will never work with you," I said, full of revulsion.

"Because I lied to you," she said. "Not because I'm not right."

"You're *not* right."

"It's easy to feel pious and moral when you're sitting on the sidelines."

"I haven't been . . ."

"In Nova Scotia, you will be. Grace, I know you. You're a good person. The kind we need more of. And you can sit back and let less-moral people make these tough decisions, or you can stay and try to make better ones yourself. And maybe you'll make some mistakes, maybe you can't save everyone . . . but I think you can do some real good. More than you'd be doing by running away." I remembered how recently I'd urged Father Dennehy to do this very thing—to be a moral counter to Dawn's desperation. If he wasn't up for the task . . . was I?

I stared her down. "Who are you? Your organization. Who are you even asking me to help?"

"Jude must have told you there are lots of people like me, all over the world," she said. "All different religions, all different backgrounds, all united with one goal."

"Yeah."

"We're trying to make the world the way it was."

Full of death and war and destruction? I couldn't mask my horror. "Why would you want to do that?"

"Because it's better than the world we have now. Trust me. You're young enough that you don't know any different, but believe me . . . this world is not a happy one. Even if it seems to be."

"You keep saying you're the right side. Why should I believe that?"

She was unequivocal. "Because Prophet Joshua is evil."

A shiver ran down my spine. "What do you mean?"

"You met him. You can't tell? The man is obsessed with power."

"He already has plenty," I argued.

"How do you think he got it?" she asked. "That technology he's working on? Just the tip of the iceberg. Imagine if he's not just Punishing you for your thoughts. Imagine if he can control them. If he remains unchecked, many more innocent people are going to get hurt."

I couldn't believe I was even considering it. "So what happens if I stay?"

"Like I said, Joshua's people want to see what you're up to. There will be someone following your every move, listening to everything you say."

"That guard guy, right?"

She hesitated. And then I guess she figured I'd know sooner or later. "Not the guard. It'll be Zack Cannon." The way she said it, like she knew about him, I realized Jude must have told her everything. "Just because you know him, that doesn't make him any less dangerous. It makes him more dangerous."

"Can I make him go away?"

"Convince him you're loyal to the prophet. Convince him you don't know anything."

"I can't. Zack already knows." I briefly explained about Macy. Dawn didn't seem concerned.

"He knows you know about the pills. But he doesn't know you're working with us."

"No, but Zack knows a different story than I told the prophet, he knows I saw him in the woods. If he tells someone, and it gets back to Joshua . . ."

"He hasn't told anyone," Dawn said. "If he had, you'd be dead right now."

"So what? I'm off the hook?"

"You could be. Convince him you won't be any trouble. Convince him you're not worth watching anymore."

I tried to think of all the things I still didn't know. "Who does Zack work for? The prophet?"

"Not directly, but yes."

"What is his organization, what does it do?" As she hesitated, I prodded her, "What happened to telling me everything?"

"Zack's job is to help keep the illusion that we're living in Great Spirit's paradise. I don't know how much you know about brain chemistry . . ."

"More than I did a couple weeks ago."

"Not everyone feels guilt," she explained. "Sociopaths, for example—when they do something you and I might think was wrong, they feel nothing. Zack identifies those people and removes them from the general population, where they could confuse others. Not to mention the heinous acts those people might commit without consequences to restrain them."

"Ciaran," I realized. "That's why he was never Punished."

Dawn had clearly heard the story from Jude, and nodded. "Exactly like Ciaran."

"So all of those people in that prison? The ones who weren't scientists?"

"Were they sociopaths? A lot of them, yes."

I was glad I hadn't known that at the time. It would have been even more chilling walking those dimly lit aisles.

"I'll be honest—when Jude brought you to me, I didn't want to save you."

I didn't hide my disdain. "I remember."

"The reason I changed my mind was anticipating a moment like this. We've spent years trying to make headway against the prophet, with no success. Helping you was a risk, yes. But if you do what I think you can do? If you remain our spy within the prophet's army, if you do more of what you did to get us to West Virginia? You'll turn the tide of this war and end it forever."

A terrible thought occurred to me. "If Zack is following me, I couldn't see Jude."

"No. It wouldn't be safe. But if we win, this all ends. You could live a normal life. You wouldn't have to run, you wouldn't be risking your lives, or the lives of those you love."

"Those we love?"

"What do you think would happen if you made a wrong move, if someone found you in Nova Scotia? It's not just your life, it's your father's. Your friends'."

"You're saying I'm safer if I stay."

"Not at all. I'm saying your life makes a difference if you stay." She'd come to the end of her pitch. "Think about it."

She stepped away, leaving me once again with more questions than answers. My mind was swimming, overwhelmed, and for the first time in a long time, I took a deep breath, and I prayed. I asked Great Spirit what to do. The real Great Spirit, the one I still believed watched over me from above, even if He didn't have any power to affect things on Earth. The one who'd spoken to me days earlier through that uneasy feeling in my gut, telling me something was wrong with our rescue mission. I needed the same kind of guidance now. What would Great Spirit do? Help Dawn's group of rebels, help people see the truth? Help everyone be free, help them live happier lives, prevent scenes like that black market massacre? Or flee the country and lick His wounds? I had to decide now. The clock was ticking.

But I didn't move. As alluring as a life on the run with Jude sounded . . . it turns out I wasn't just a simple teenage girl who wanted a simple life. Maybe I wanted to be something more. Something I'd never even considered until that instant. All that time I'd spent volunteering in Haiti, ministering to Outcasts . . . that was me trying to make a difference, trying to help humanity, trying to make my life mean something. And now, I was being given a chance to do that. No matter how idyllic the life I created for myself might be, I knew I'd never truly be happy unless I was doing something meaningful. And while no voice spoke down at me from on high, the knowledge came from within. I didn't know if I could trust Dawn. But I had to pick a side. I had to try to help.

# CHAPTER 14

As the end-of-school bell rang, I followed a chattering Macy out the door. She'd finally gotten the courage to confide her story to one of our other friends—her fear of stigma outweighed by the desire to tell everyone that she'd been cured by the prophet himself. Everyone oohed and aahed as she recounted his healing touch. "I thought he was going to tell me I'd sinned too much, but he didn't. He told me Great Spirit loved me, and that everything was going to be okay. And then . . ." She looked up, noticing. "What's my brother doing here?"

She pointed to a car I recognized as Zack's. The windows were tinted—I couldn't see inside. She waved to him. "Zack!"

He got out of the car, smiled, approached us. "Figured you've had a rough week—I thought you'd like door-to-door service."

Macy hugged him. "Thanks."

"I promised Mom and Dad I wouldn't tease you anymore, but that doesn't mean I can't tell you that you look ridiculous in those sunglasses."

Macy shoved him playfully. "Lies."

"Everyone knows what you look like, you're just drawing attention."

"Three different people said I look like a movie star."

"Sure, the star of a monster movie."

As they bickered their way to the car, Zack looked back to me. "Want a ride home?" I shook my head. "Come on, I'm driving right by your house. Why waste all that time on the bus?"

"I'm fine."

Zack was getting frustrated. "Grace, just get in the car."

I took a deep breath. This was the shape of things to come, wasn't it? "Okay."

Zack tried to pull me into casual conversation, and I managed the best I could. It occurred to me now that maybe Zack wasn't a killer—as far as I could tell, his only victim had turned up alive. But still, he was watching me, knowingly making me a prisoner in my own day-to-day life. I still wanted to be as far away from him as possible.

The car was still rolling to a stop in front of my house as I opened the door, said my quickest goodbye, and bolted inside. I watched Zack drive away. At this moment, I was out of sight, but from what Dawn had said, he'd still be tracking my phone, my dad's car. For all I knew, my whole house was bugged now. I had to live every moment from now on like I was in Prophet Joshua's office.

And I couldn't meet Jude, I couldn't even say a real goodbye. The guilt weighed on me, heavy and permanent. I'd been so furious at Jude for abandoning me, and here I was doing the same to him. Worse, because I'd chosen to leave him behind. Right now, he was excitedly waiting for me at our meeting point. Soon he would begin to worry, wondering why I was running late. And eventually Dawn would tell him that I simply wasn't coming. I knew how I'd feel, if he'd put me in that position—it would be the end of our relationship, maybe even our friendship, forever.

I thought back on everything I'd just experienced. The close shaves with Joshua and Samuel. Friends brought back from the brink of death. Enemies who couldn't be. An army of sociopaths still sitting in that prison. All those scientists, who had chosen potential suicide over the certainty of a lifetime of captivity . . . I wondered if, wherever they were now, they were happy they'd taken that path.

I remembered when my path had been simple. When the way I judged people had been simple. Outcasts bad, cute boys good. How easy my life had been then. But in a way, that ease had felt hollow, meaningless. In a perfect world, what is there to strive for? At least now maybe I could do something that actually mattered.

I considered what my future might look like. Working for the prophet, my every move scrutinized by all sides. Did I see an end to this? Even if I spent the rest of my high school and college years saving lives, I couldn't imagine being happy. I'd be doing all that alone, with no one to share it with. But maybe that wasn't the point. Maybe I didn't get to be one of the happy ones. Maybe in exchange for living a life that was about something, I had to give up all the happy things in it. Maybe, even if I couldn't find comfort, I could find meaning. I'd have to.

Instead of living for myself, I could live for my father, for my friends at school, for the memory of my mother. The Revelations had taken her from me, but I knew the nanotech living in our brains would take many more mothers, many more children, until I did something to stop it. And I would. I was certain of it.

You're laughing at me. Grace Luther, rotting in her prison cell, looking back on her youth and trying to give her life significance. But I do see meaning in it. Despite all the tragedies that had already occurred, and were yet to come . . . I know I did everything I could to squeeze value out of my little life. And whatever mistakes I've made, Great Spirit's opinion is the only one I put any stock in. Because if I've learned anything, it's this. You're wrong. You're wrong about everything. I was wrong almost every step of the way, and you're all wrong to judge me for it. We were all wrong to put our trust in leaders who lied to us, we were all wrong to think we knew what was right. But someday, at Great Spirit's Great Judgment, we'll know the truth. I'll see you then.

# ACKNOWLEDGMENTS

First off, my parents, to whom this novel is dedicated: this book would not exist without all of your emotional, financial, and creative support over the past few decades. You were my first editors, my first cheerleaders, my first champions. Dad, thank you for the six thousand times you talked me out of giving up. Mom, for reading all the stories I wrote as a teenager, even the most embarrassingly bad ones, and always encouraging me to keep writing and revising. Dave, for buying stock in me all those years ago. I am indebted to all of you more than words can say.

Thank you to the immensely hard-working Randy Kiyan for getting this book into the right hands, and to Claire Abramowitz for passing it along—it never would have seen the light of day without either of you.

To my amazing book agent Peter Steinberg—your thoughtful notes and excellent salesmanship not only got this book sold, but launched my career.

To Rebecca Lucash, my first editor at Harper Voyager, for

all of your insights that took this story to the next level. And to David Pomerico, Priyanka Krishnan, and the rest of the Harper Voyager team, for all your help with this series. It's been such a pleasure working with all of you, and I'm excited we get to do two more of these together!

To Ari Levinson, whose thoughts and ideas permeate every page of this book. Thank you for helping me build this world, for your feedback on countless drafts, and for your support every single day throughout this process.

To everyone else who read early drafts: Ann Acacia Kim, Alex Smith, Amy Thurlow, Alex Spear, Alison Kane, Brad Riddell, Sue Amy, Cathy Hill, Laura Herb, Sarah Hawley, Linda Johnson Tarkoff . . . It is no easy feat to trudge through a rough draft by a first-time novelist, and your input was enormously valuable. And an additional thanks to the many friends who gave input earlier in the process, as I was developing the story and the world.

To Markus Plank, for advising me on neuroscience, helping to ground the sci-fi tech in some kind of reality. Apologies for anything I still messed up.

To Yuval Harari, who has no idea who I am, but whose *Brief History of Humankind* inspired quite a bit of my favorite dialogue.

To the incredibly talented Eva, who inspired me to write a novel in the first place.

And to all the rest of my friends, family, teachers, and mentors, for all of your support along the way. I am immensely lucky to have all of you in my life.

## ABOUT THE AUTHOR

Sarah Tarkoff currently writes for the CW series *Arrow*. Other TV writing credits include ABC's *Mistresses*, Lifetime's *Witches of East End*, and the animated series *Vixen* and *The Ray*. She graduated from the University of Southern California with a degree in screenwriting (hence all the screenwriting), and currently lives in Los Angeles. *Sinless* is her debut novel.